## "I need a personnel manager. Not a mistress."

Gareth continued curtly. "My offer was exactly as I made it. And I resent the accusation that I'm lying."

Roxane shrugged. "You've lied to me before, you know."

Incredibly, he looked genuinely baffled. "What are you talking about?"

"Don't you remember?" she said bitterly. "I and fifty others worked for you at head office. When the rumors started about the move, your manager deliberately told us it wouldn't happen. Presumably to give us a false sense of security. And it worked."

"Oh. Yes, I see." Then he said softly. "I didn't actually lie to you, you know. Nobody asked *me*."

"And if you had been asked? Would you have told the truth?" Roxane held her breath...and wondered why Gareth's answer meant so very much to her.

**KAY GREGORY** is a new author. This book is her second romance for Harlequin. She is married, lives in Canada and has two grown-up sons.

# KAY GREGORY

## no way to say goodbye

### *Harlequin Books*

TORONTO • NEW YORK • LONDON
AMSTERDAM • PARIS • SYDNEY • HAMBURG
STOCKHOLM • ATHENS • TOKYO • MILAN

To my sons Nathan and Adrian,
with love and gratitude
for all their support, knowledge and help
with the background to my books.

Harlequin Presents first edition August 1989
ISBN 0-373-11191-6

Original hardcover edition published in 1988
by Mills & Boon Limited

# CHAPTER ONE

A WARM, masculine hand fell lightly on Roxane's shoulder, and she started up from her chair as a deep voice behind her said crisply, 'Get a move on please, Miss Peters. The meeting's about to begin.'

Roxane gulped and looked guiltily into eyes that were deep-set, very dark, and fixed on her with such commanding intensity that she put her hand awkwardly to her face to hide an incipient blush.

'Yes, Mr Mardon,' she replied hastily, scuttling away from his look with an embarrassment which surprised her as much as it annoyed her.

She had been attempting to finish proof-reading the new personnel manual which Annette, her boss, had wanted back yesterday, and in her enthusiasm she had quite forgotten the employees' meeting that had been called for eleven o'clock. It must be an important one, she thought, for the president to have taken the trouble to summon her personally.

Flustered, breathless and last as usual, Roxane hurried into the boardroom and sank as unobtrusively as possible into the remaining vacant chair.

She glanced quickly around the room and saw that nearly all of the fifty-odd employees of the Vancouver office of Dart Express Delivery were draped against the walls or seated at the long, coffee-stained table. And all the faces expressed the same mild curiosity, tempered with irritation at having their work—or coffee-breaks—interrupted.

Annette, Dart's personnel manager, was conducting the meeting, but as Roxane waited for her boss to speak, she was still remembering the surprisingly warm and pleasant touch of Mr Mardon's hand on her shoulder. She noticed the way Annette's tongue passed hesitantly over her lips—but she was not really concentrating on her words—which made the shock even greater when the strangled gasps all around her brought her rapidly back to her surroundings, and she heard Annette say gruffly, 'So I've been asked to tell you that our Vancouver head office is moving to Toronto.'

She spoke baldly, with a blank, set face and no attempt at softening platitudes. 'The Toronto office opens tomorrow, I'm afraid. Which means you've all been let go, so . . .' she shrugged and concluded in a rush, 'so you can collect your things and go home now. If there are any questions, Mr Mardon may be here to answer them tomorrow. Of course you'll be receiving payment in lieu of notice, and all the holiday pay you're entitled to, and—well, I guess that's it.'

Annette's solid face had gone very white, and she held her well-endowed figure rigidly straight. She was fidgeting with a piece of paper which she kept pulling between her fingers.

For a moment there was a dead, shattered silence in the room. Roxane's gaze moved from one stunned face to the next, finally coming to rest again on Annette—who wouldn't meet her eyes.

Big Molly in the corner, her small eyes glistening suspiciously, asked quickly, 'Why are *you* the one to tell us, Annette? Didn't Mr Mardon have the guts?'

Annette cleared her throat, opened her mouth, shuffled her feet and then muttered something unconvincing about Mr Mardon having thought it might be easier if the news came from the personnel manager as they all knew her so well . . . Her voice trailed off, and she turned towards the door.

'Annette,' called Roxane, her light brown hair flying forward over her shoulders as her voice halted the personnel manager in her tracks. 'Annette, why did you lie to us when the rumours started? The rumours about the move? You said it was all nonsense, and that of course head office wasn't moving. Why weren't we told the truth and given some reasonable notice?'

Annette did not turn around, and her voice was tight and muffled. 'Yes. I'm sorry about that. But—Mr Mardon thought it would be easier this way—for everybody.'

'For himself, you mean,' scoffed Molly. 'And I suppose *you're* going to Toronto too, aren't you, Annette?'

'Yes. Yes, I am. I and a few others.'

Not many others, thought Roxane, glancing around the room. Most of the staff were in here—being fired with brutal insensitivity by a personnel manager who had about as much tact as a combat tank. If Mr Mardon honestly thought they would prefer the news to come this way, he must be a very poor judge of character. Not that she really believed he cared how his employees took the bombshell. He just wanted to get it over with, with as little inconvenience to himself as possible.

Her eyes moved to Molly, who had started to heave herself up from her position against the wall. She doubted if Molly was right about Mr Mardon, though.

Callous he might be. All too obviously *was*. But gutless? She didn't know him well, and what she did know she didn't much like—but of one thing she was certain. That virile, masterful hunk with the deep-set, gloriously brooding eyes was *not,* not even remotely, likely to lack courage. For some reason she was not prepared to analyse, Roxane would almost have staked her fortune on that. Which, she admitted ruefully, was a safe bet anyway, as she didn't have a fortune to stake.

Her mind returned abruptly to the present, as she realised that everyone was shuffling to their feet now. Bewildered eyes met hers and passed on. Jerry, the office boy, laughed nervously, and elderly Martha, who was nearing retirement, began to sniff audibly.

Slowly the beginnings of something that was more than just bewilderment began to stir in Roxane's semi-paralysed brain. She saw the confused, stricken faces of the friends she had worked with for three and a half years as they all drifted dazedly out of the boardroom. Martha was crying openly. At her age she would never find another job. Molly at least was young and energetic, but she had little training in anything useful, and had been lucky to find her job in the mailroom at Dart. Then there was Lisa. She was a single parent with three small children to support. And Art from accounting had an invalid wife. Jerry, who was performing a little dance and throwing spitballs with a rubber band, would be all right though. Watching him, Roxane felt almost inclined to smile for the first time since Annette had broken the news. The world would never defeat the effervescent Jerry for long.

Then she looked at the other faces, and her smile faded.

In the outer office the distraught group of ex-employees came to a confused, milling halt. Annette, who was in front of them, turned around.

'Get your things and leave as quickly as possible,' she said abruptly, with her eyes fixed well above their heads. And then, as Roxane crossed the large room, sat down at her desk and began to tidy the sheets of the new personnel manual, she added loudly, 'No, leave that, Roxane. Just leave everything where it is.'

Leave this, leave that. Roxane shrugged, deliberately spread the papers into a disorganised mess across the desk, and started to turn out drawers. All around her she heard other drawers opening and closing, nervous mutters, and from Martha's office, the sound of a nose being much too forcefully blown.

Bastard, she thought, pushing her big, black glasses irritably up her nose. Lovely to look at Mr Mardon may be, but he's still a callous, unfeeling bastard. He doesn't give a damn about any of us. So it suits him to have the head office in Toronto—he'll probably make more money there, as if he needs it. But he hasn't even the human decency to give us reasonable notice. In spite of all the work and effort most of us have been putting in for years. In the end, what thanks did we get? Her glasses slipped, and she shoved them in place again. Just severance pay and Annette telling us to get out quickly.

Yes, Annette. Not for the first time, it occurred to Roxane that as a manager of people, Annette was the worst choice Mr Mardon could have made. The buxom blonde had been an employee-relations disaster ever since she had received the appointment nine months ago. In fact, thought Roxane, not to put too fine a point on it, and not even to blow my own horn, personnel would have gone up in flames ages ago if I hadn't been here to provide a smoke-screen for Annette's incompetence. And that man had actually had the insensitivity to give the woman the job of telling his staff that Dart no longer needed them.

With an exasperated snort, Roxane flung tissues, magazines, her letter opener, coffee mug and a miscellaneous collection of personal debris into a tattered plastic bag she found at the bottom of the drawer. Then she stood up, paused, bent down again and added a year's supply of Dart's pens, pencils and Scotch tape to the pile. It wouldn't make a bit of difference to the company's continued success, but somehow this act of larcenous defiance made her feel just a little bit less of a patsy.

Hefting the bag under one arm, she walked out to the centre of the office.

One or two people, looking pale and tight-lipped, had already left the building and were walking rapidly towards their cars. Beyond them through the windows Roxane saw dark clouds hovering around the control tower of Vancouver International Airport, and she wondered vaguely if she would ever look at it from quite this angle again.

In the middle of the floor of the main accounting office, small groups of workers stood about murmuring to each other, exchanging phone numbers and exclaiming in disbelief that this couldn't really be happening to them.

Roxane joined Lisa, Molly and Martha in a huddle outside the computer room.

'Well,' said Lisa, chewing resignedly at a large wad of gum, 'Canada Manpower next port-of-call. Again. Just when I thought I finally had a chance to get my life back on track. Stupid thing is, I turned down a job offer last week. I felt Dart had been good to me, and it didn't seem fair to let them down with such short notice.'

'Huh. More fool you,' grunted Molly. 'But the writing was on the wall, wasn't it? I guess we were all just too dumb to see it.'

'I don't know,' argued Roxane. 'It's not dumb to be loyal—or to trust your employer. No one expects to be lied to.'

'No,' agreed Lisa. 'But we will from now on.'

Roxane nodded thoughtfully. 'I know,' she agreed. 'That's just the trouble. And I resent being turned into a cynic by a snake like Mr Mardon.' But even as she said it, she knew she felt more than just resentment. For a few minutes this morning she had actually been day-dreaming about that heartless hunk, and now she was furious with herself for being even superficially attracted to him.

Then she realised that Martha was tugging at her arm and nodding towards a small, grim-faced group by the front door. Mr Mardon, Annette and four other people who wouldn't meet their eyes.

'They must be the ones who are going to Toronto,' whispered Martha.

'Yes. And they're watching us like hawks to make sure we don't try to take revenge,' said Roxane perceptively.

'Revenge?'

'Mm. You know. Attack the computer with a meat-axe. Set fire to the invoice files. That sort of thing.'

'We don't have a meat-axe,' sighed Molly regretfully. 'Anyone got a match?'

Roxane laughed and the group by the door stiffened suspiciously.

'I think they want us to go,' suggested Martha.

'Well, they can't throw us out bodily,' said Molly. 'Even Mr Mardon would have trouble slinging *me* over his shoulder.'

'Perhaps,' agreed Lisa, giving the large young woman a watery smile. 'All the same—I don't want to hang around any longer anyway, do you? Let's get out of here.'

'Yes, let's.' With one accord the four of them made for the door, and Roxane saw that they were the last ones left in the building.

Story of my life, she thought to herself. And then, as they approached the group by the exit, it occurred to her that even if she wasn't about to assault the computer with a meat-axe, she was certainly not above putting a wrench in Mr Mardon's well-oiled gears. After all, why make things easy for him?

Lisa, Molly and Martha filed hurriedly through the door. Roxane, hanging back, put her hand on the handle, and then stopped. Turning around, she batted her long brown lashes at the president, giggled inanely and murmured, 'Oh, dear. Silly me. I do believe I have to pay a visit before I go.'

Mr Mardon gave her a long, hard stare and didn't trouble to reply, but as she tripped back across the length of the room, she could almost feel those deep eyes boring into her back.

Once safely in the Ladies, she rested her hands on the sink and stared at herself in the mirror. The soft brown hair that usually fell in a smooth sheet to her shoulders were hanging untidily over her face, completely hiding the big, amber-coloured eyes that in any case were obscured by the over-sized frames of her glasses. Her cheeks were lit by two angry streaks of pink.

I'll fix him, she thought grimly. His clean sweep of Dart employees is going to take *much* longer than he expects.

Carefully removing the glasses to reveal the attractive lines of her small, oval face, she spent the next fifteen minutes slowly applying powder, mascara, eyeshadow and lipstick. She was just adding a touch of scent to her wrists when the door behind her shuddered as a fist crashed into it and a man's voice thundered rudely, 'Open up, Miss Peters. You've had plenty of time to powder that charming nose of yours, and it's time to get the hell out.'

Roxane glanced at the still vibrating door, and her eye caught the sudden glitter of a wisp of leftover festive tinsel stuck on one of the hinges. It was the second week in January, but the lingering remnants of Christmas had evidently not quite vanished from the office.

Christmas! Huh. Bah, humbug, thought Roxane disgustedly. Thanks for the seasonal spirit, Mr Mardon.

His fist was hammering on the door again. 'Miss Peters,' he shouted, the deep voice sounding as though it meant business. 'Miss Peters, do you hear me?'

'Yes, Mr Mardon,' Roxane cooed sweetly. 'I'll only be a minute.' Her eye fell on the tinsel again, and suddenly she reached for a paper cup and filled it to the brim with cold water. Holding her bag in one hand and the paper cup in the other, she headed carefully for the door.

'Mr Mardon,' she called, in the most dulcet tones she could summon up, 'Mr Mardon, *would* you mind opening the door for me? I seem to be overloaded. Oh, thank you,' she gushed, as the door immediately swung open and she found herself gazing into stormy dark eyes that glared furiously at her from under thick, well-shaped black brows. 'Thank you so much, Mr Mardon.'

'You are *not* particularly welcome.' His voice grated out from rigidly compressed lips, and Roxane swallowed and then was furious with herself because now, for the first time since Mr Mardon had taken over Dart nine months ago, she found herself noticing those lips. They were firm, full, very sensuous, just the kind of lips she liked on a man . . .

No. No way. Not on this man, she didn't. Not when he could cold-heartedly fire fifty employees without even a thought for their feelings, their past loyalty or their futures.

'Now if you have *quite* finished, Miss Peters,' he was saying sarcastically, 'perhaps you could manage to leave us.'

Roxane gave him her best girlish grin, chirped, 'Of course, Mr Mardon,' tripped daintily over her own feet and arched the entire contents of the paper cup in a cold, wet stream down his face.

'Oh, I'm *so* sorry,' she burbled. 'I just don't know how that could have happened, Mr Mardon. Are you sure you're all right?'

'No,' he said, in a dangerously controlled voice, as the water glistened on his lightly tanned skin. 'No, Miss Peters, the only thing I am sure of is that if you're not out of here in ten seconds flat, you're going to wish very much that you were.'

Roxane looked at the lean, muscular body looming above her in that oh-so-well-fitting suit, and calculated the strength of the powerful arm that was wiping a handkerchief around the wet, rugged contours of his face and neck. She decided that discretion was the better part of valour.

'Yes, Mr Mardon,' she babbled. 'Of course. I'm so sorry, my fault entirely . . .'

'Miss Peters . . .' His voice interrupted her, low and smooth like bladed steel.

Roxane took one look at the smouldering eyes fastened on her face, saw him take a step towards her, and fled.

As the cold air outside struck her face, she drew in her breath and gasped. Had that been a close shave, or had that been a close shave? She was already scrambling into the front seat of her bright red Honda before it occurred to her that there was nothing, legally, that Mr Mardon could have done to her, even though he was obviously quite well aware that she had thrown that water on purpose. But then she had a feeling that legality had never been too important to the president of Dart Express Delivery.

It was only as she pulled into the car park of her apartment in Marpole, just across the Oak Street Bridge, that she remembered the way he had looked at her in that moment before she had run away. The dark eyes had been angry, all right; furious, in fact. But behind the anger there had been . . . speculation? Appreciation? No, it couldn't have been that. But something very—seductive. Something that, maddeningly in the present circumstances, she had a feeling she would not forget.

Roxane watched as her room-mate dumped a load of

groceries on to the kitchen counter, paused suddenly, and turned sharply around.

'What are *you* doing home so early?' exclaimed Nina. 'You *never* get in before me.'

'I do now,' replied Roxane. 'In fact I'm permanently "in".'

Nina's blue eyes widened and her blonde curls formed a waving halo around her head as she lifted it to stare at her friend in astonishment. 'What on earth do you mean? You haven't quit, have you?'

'No.' Roxane told her what had happened.

'Well, I'll be damned.' Nina sat down abruptly on a white plastic chair that creaked alarmingly under the onslaught. 'I'm going to have to lose weight,' she remarked irrelevantly—and for at least the fifth time that week.

'Or we'll have to get a new chair,' grinned Roxane.

'All very well for you. You always stay five foot six and slim.'

'Well, you stay five foot six.'

Nina threw a cushion at her. 'Thanks,' she muttered. 'Oh, Roxie, why are we discussing my weight and the furniture when we should be talking about your job?'

'Because it's much less traumatic. And I don't have a job to discuss.'

'That's just it. What are you going to do?' She looked suddenly stricken. 'You're not going back to Winnipeg, are you? To live with your parents, I mean. Or your brother?'

'No,' said Roxane positively. 'I came out here to get away from snow in flat places. Snow belongs on mountains. For the exclusive benefit of skiers.'

'If you haven't got a job, you can't afford to ski,

though,' Nina pointed out prosaically.

'I'll get a job.' Roxane jumped up from the long, angular couch with its pattern of clashing greens and mauves, and started to pace rapidly around the room.

'Watch your glasses,' shrieked Nina.

'What? Oh.' Roxane bent down to retrieve the big frames lying an inch from her toes on the purple rug.

'Why on earth don't you wear your contacts?' asked Nina irritably. 'You're always leaving those things on the floor. And then when I squash them flat one day, you'll say it's all my fault.'

'No, I won't. But you're right. I can forget about the glasses for a while.' She wandered into the bathroom and began to insert contacts with a dexterity born of long practice.

'Bastard,' she remarked to no one in particular.

'What was that?' called Nina.

'I said "bastard". Mr Mardon.'

'Oh. He is, isn't he. Why do you suppose he did it?'

'I guess he wanted to move head office to Toronto because it's the centre of the business community. And when he calls managers' meetings, a central location makes more sense financially. I don't really blame him for the move. He always knows what he's doing. Dart was going downhill fast when he bought it out nine months ago, and he turned things around almost right away.'

'How? By firing staff?'

'Mm. Partly, I'm afraid.' Roxane turned her head to stare thoughtfully into the mirror. 'But some of the managers in the branches across Canada weren't doing much of a job, so I can't really fault him on that, either. Like everything else, a courier service has to be efficient or it doesn't stay in business for long.'

'You'd think the old partners would have realised that.'

'Yes, but that was just it. They *were* getting old—and tired. They were ready to sell out—and Mr Mardon was looking for something to do with his money, I think.'

Nina stood up and followed Roxane into the bathroom where she was restoring her contact lens case to the cupboard. 'Where did he make his money?' she asked idly.

'Don't know. Rumour has it that his origins are a bit shady, and that he made it all by gambling.'

'Is rumour reliable?'

'Probably not.'

'Oh. Well, I suppose it doesn't matter now, does it? But I still don't see why he didn't play fair with you all.'

'Neither do I. Don't suppose it occurred to him.'

'Huh. Suppose not,' grunted Nina, adding irrelevantly that she wished she could improve her figure as easily as Roxane improved her face by removing her glasses.

Roxane laughed. 'Your figure's just fine,' she assured her.

'Sure. There's just too much of it.'

They had been having the same argument ever since they met head-on on the ski slopes and moved in together a few weeks after Roxane arrived in Vancouver. As always, it ended in mutual agreement to change the subject.

'This is the wrong evening for me to be going out,' said Nina now. 'I mean—I shouldn't leave you alone after a shock like you've had today. But Jack's coming for me in a little while, and I can't get hold of him to put him off.'

'No reason why you should,' said Roxane quickly. 'I shall have a lovely evening planning my next job—and thinking black thoughts about Mr Mardon.' She giggled. 'You should have seen his face when I poured that water on him.'

'I wish I had. Roxie . . .?'

'Mm.'

'Is he married?'

'Who, Mr Mardon? No, he isn't. I shouldn't think any woman would have him—even if he is a hunk. There are rumours that he's having a steaming affair with Annette, though. I think she came out from Toronto with him.'

'Is that why she got the personnel manager's job?'

'Probably. Mr Mardon knows incompetence when he sees it. But in this case there were—mitigating circumstances.' Her lip curved in a sneer. 'Why do you ask, Nina?'

'No reason. Just wondered.' Nina sauntered into her bedroom, pulled a jacket out of the wardrobe and inspected herself anxiously in the mirror. It wasn't true that she had had no reason for asking about Mr Mardon's marital state. Because for all Roxane's contempt, Nina had a feeling there was more behind her room-mate's anger than the fact that she had unfairly lost her job. Nina hadn't lived with Roxane for three years without learning to read the signs of a more than casual interest in a man. Although this time it was obvious that any attraction Roxane might feel for her ex-president was going nowhere—fast.

A few minutes later Nina's current boyfriend arrived to take her out. Roxane smiled as she watched them leave. They were gazing soulfully into each other's eyes, and Jack's arm was possessively and proudly around his lady's waist. It looked as though this most recent of many liaisons might prove more serious than the rest. Roxane hoped so, for Nina's sake, because she knew her friend had a genuine, if quite unwarranted, complex about her weight, and was afraid no man would ever take her seriously.

After they left, Roxane changed into jeans, thumped herself down on the couch and pulled a pad of paper towards her. Tomorrow she would visit the unemployment offices, but right now it was time to make a list of possible jobs. She picked up a pencil.

And then the phone calls started.

First it was Martha who wanted a sympathetic ear. Then Molly, who had moved fast and been turned down for two jobs already. After that it was Lisa, almost in tears as the full realisation of the disaster that had struck her began to hit home. Her call was followed by other equally distraught voices belonging to the friendly, and mainly happy-go-lucky people Roxane had known and worked with for the last three and a half years. She had been fond of all of them, and for many it was going to be tough to find another job.

By the time the last caller hung up at half-past ten, Roxane felt drained, drooping, depressed and, as she sank back against the couch, more and more angry with the man who had caused all this distress. As she had told Nina, she didn't fault him for wanting to make the move. But it would not have hurt him to give them proper notice, instead of lying when the inevitable rumours started. That way some of them, like Lisa, would already have found jobs by now. Others, such as Martha, would at least have been prepared, and perhaps spent a little less of their hard-earned cash at Christmas. And none of them would have felt this sense of angry shock and betrayal that their years of hard work counted for nothing if their only reward was a curt dismissal, incredibly not from the president, but from the hopelessly inept Annette.

Roxane strummed her fingers at an increasing tempo on the green and mauve arm of the couch. She stared at the pad of paper on which she had intended to sketch job possibilities and thought that at the moment she would much prefer to sketch pictures of G.M. Mardon—preferably stepping on to a scaffold with his strong hands tied securely behind his back and those very black eyes suitably covered by a blindfold.

Then another, even more satisfactory image occurred to her—of that lean, hard-looking body stretched out naked on a rack . . .

Yes. Well, never mind about his body; that was no concern of hers.

She remembered his face with the water dripping down it and those definitely unblinded eyes glaring furiously into hers. Altogether a much more comforting picture. Roxane smiled waspishly.

All the same, it wasn't right. He shouldn't be allowed to get away with such brutal back-stabbing, and pay no greater penalty than a momentary cold shower outside the Ladies.

Her eye fell on one of the daily papers, the *Vancouver Enquirer*. Across the front page was a large black headline announcing the demise of a well-known British Columbia company which had gone out of business because the president had been caught with his hand in the shareholders' pockets. Below that, in not much smaller letters, was an item about a sex-ring in a local junior school. Sex and scandal. The *Enquirer's* bread and butter . . . Hmm.

No, she couldn't do much about the sex. Bed and breakfast with Annette just wouldn't pique the interest of the jaded gentlemen of the newsroom. But scandal now, real or imagined, human tragedy, desperate families thrown on the dole . . .

Thoughtfully Roxane hauled the telephone off the floor, placed it on her knees and began to dial.

'I'd like the night news desk, please,' she said crisply, when a sleepy voice answered her call.

'Certainly, miss. Hold on.'

A moment later a much more alert voice came on the line, and by the time she hung up the phone, Roxane's soft, generous lips were no longer drooping, but curved in the satisfied smile of a cat who thinks his dreams of the family canary are about to come true at last.

# CHAPTER TWO

WHEN Roxane returned from the unemployment office early the following afternoon, she could hear the phone ringing before she put the key in the lock. But inevitably, after banging her ankle on the sharp-edged coffee-table that Nina had made at school, the moment she lifted the receiver she heard the line go dead.

'Ouch,' she muttered, rubbing her bruised ankle. Oh, well, it couldn't have been about a job anyway, because she had no interviews scheduled until tomorrow.

When it rang again fifteen minutes later, she skirted the coffee-table carefully and took her time about answering.

'Miss Peters?' The rough, very masculine voice sent a small thrill down her spine before she even realised who was speaking.

'Miss Peters?' the voice repeated, when Roxane did not reply immediately. Now there was a hard edge of impatience crackling across the wires. Roxane opened her mouth, closed it again, wound the cord around her fist—and found herself unable to utter a word.

'All right.' He was resigned. 'If that's the way you want it, I can play games too.'

'I—I'm not—playing games, Mr Mardon,' she managed to croak out at last.

'No? You could have fooled me. Now Miss Peters, since you appear to have found your tongue, perhaps you'll be good enough to tell me what the hell you mean by going to the papers.'

'Paper,' corrected Roxane, beginning to get a grip on herself. 'Just one. The *Enquirer*.'

There was an exasperated growl at the other end of the line. 'And that *one* is quite enough, isn't it, Miss Peters? Vancouver's daily dose of sex, sleaze and slander. Very stimulating in their places, I don't doubt. The first two, at least. But all I need right now is my name splashed across the front page of that rag, and Dart's business will drop overnight.'

'Precisely,' said Roxane, not bothering to disguise her jubilation.

She heard him draw in his breath. 'All right,' he said, in a voice which was now ice-cold and dangerous. 'All right, Miss Peters, so you want to destroy my business. Well, you can take it from me that you haven't a hope in hell. I hold all the cards, I'm afraid, and I'm not about to be pushed around by a pretty pipsqueak in glasses the size of grapefruits.'

'Grapefruits?' choked Roxane, momentarily diverted from her satisfaction that she had succeeded in denting his armour, and fighting a totally unexpected urge to laugh. 'Did you say grapefruits?'

'I did.' Just for a moment she thought she heard an answering hint of laughter in his voice, but then it was gone as he went on bitingly, 'I understand the *Enquirer* intends to publish an interview with you—revealing the details of Dart's move to Toronto.'

Roxane could afford to be defiant. He was safely on the other side of the Oak Street Bridge—if he was phoning from the office. 'That's right,' she agreed smugly.

'Is it? But you don't *know* the details, do you Miss Peters? That's why the *Enquirer* has asked for an interview with me as well. They want to talk to us both —together.'

'Together?' Roxane was croaking again.

'That's what I said. Nice and—intimate.' His voice curled round the word insultingly. 'And then they want to publish a two-page spread, with your story on one side—and my response on the other.'

'Oh.'

'Yes, oh. And I don't know about you, Miss Peters, but I don't want that story to appear. Even though the interview would afford me the delightful opportunity to wring your pretty neck.'

There was something so calmly businesslike about the way he said it that Roxane almost believed he meant it. He had already shown himself to be without pity. No doubt he was also capable of murder. She shivered, and the thought of that interview became suddenly less appealing.

But she was not backing down.

'It's too bad you don't want the story to appear,' she told him coldly, 'because if I have anything to do with it, the *Enquirer* will publish every dirty, damaging detail.' As she spoke, all at once the realisation of what this man had done—to her and to other more desperate cases—swept over her again in a great wave of rage, and suddenly she couldn't bear to talk to him any longer.

With a little choke of disgust, she pulled the phone from her ear as if it were going to bite her, and slammed the receiver back on to its stand.

It rang again immediately, but she ignored it and slumped down on to the couch, poking her finger savagely at a big green rose.

'Ouch,' she groaned, as the rose seemed to bite back, and she felt a stabbing pain in her knuckle.

Nursing her injured finger in one hand, and trying hard to disregard the pain in her ankle, Roxane settled herself awkwardly against the bright mauve cushions. Her eyes fastened on a picture of an orange mountain surrounded by purple spikes which Nina said matched the carpet. Orange and purple. The colours matched her mood anyway. Flaming mad, and at the same time royally glum. And all because of that man she had just hung up on. That hard-boiled, arrogant, unfeeling— and totally beautiful man.

Damn. It wasn't fair. She had worked with G.M. Mardon for nine whole months without being particularly conscious of his appeal. Oh, sure, she had noticed that he had a splendid pair of shoulders and exuded an air of almost sensual authority and power. She had noted Annette's casual comment that he seemed older than thirty-one, and had even, once or twice, thought his black eyes were strikingly attractive. But only when he happened to be around. She had never caught herself day-dreaming about him before—until yesterday. That hand on her shoulder had started something—and his unusual closeness when he had ordered her to go to the meeting. Come to think of it, that was probably it. She had never been close to him before, because he was a restless man who went away a lot on business, and when he was in Vancouver he never kept still for long. When he was forced to slow down occasionally, it was to spend time with his executive staff. Like Annette, for instance.

Annette. What on earth did he see in that bosomy,

hard-faced blonde? Yes, well, that wasn't really tough to figure out, was it? Roxane sighed, and shifted restlessly on the cushions. Anyway, it couldn't possibly matter. So Mr Mardon was a sexy hunk. He was also a perfect bastard.

She sighed again. It was too bad she had broken up with Michael. The fact that there was no current man in her life made it so much easier to concentrate on rich passing beefcake—like hateful Mr Mardon. But then, in her experience, most of the nice men were poor, ordinary and, fortunately, no more inclined to fall permanently in love than she was. All the same, it would make things easier if one of her past flames were on hand at present. A little manly support would be welcome now, in view of that interview which she had no intention of avoiding. And where, like it or not, she would be faced with a very overpowering, and probably dangerously angry, president of Dart Express Delivery.

He did look quite magnificent when he was angry, as she had reason to know—with his fists bunched tight against his thighs, and those dark eyes flashing velvet flame . . .

Her reverie was interrupted abruptly as a fist which sounded anything but velvet slammed hard against the door and a harsh voice bellowed, 'Open up that door, Miss Peters. Now.'

Holding tight to the arm of the couch, Roxane stumbled to her feet as the fist crashed on to wood again. God, this man was death on doors! His bill for repairs must be unbelievable. Not that it would matter to him.

'Miss Peters,' he was shouting again. 'I told you to open the door.'

Roxane contemplated calling the police, but decided that by the time they arrived he would have the door down anyway. And her landlord, who didn't like renting to young, unmarried women, would have her and Nina out on their innocent ears in no time. Besides, she was damned if she was going to be intimidated by that handsome hulk out there. She could cope with him, or any other man.

Taking a deep breath, she crossed the room, unlocked the door and pulled it open.

The handsome hulk stepped across the threshold, yanked the door out of her hand and slammed it shut behind him. For a moment he leaned against it, breathing hard, then with one lightning movement, he had caught both her shoulders in a grip which seemed to burn her flesh, and was glaring down at her with a look that would have intimidated tougher women than Roxane.

And after that she wasn't sure that she could cope with anything any more.

The blue-black eyes raked slowly down from her hair to her chin, to her breasts and eventually almost to her feet. Then his gaze moved up again and her own eyes followed his, hypnotised by the intense, glowering scrutiny. And gradually his expression changed. A flash of—what? Astonishment?—flickered across his face.

'What is it?' she whispered. 'What's the matter?'

He shook his head, closed his eyes for a moment and then announced blankly, 'The grapefruits. They've gone.'

'What?' Roxane could not believe her ears. 'Grapefruits? What are you talking about?'

He stared at his hands, still gripping her shoulders

much too hard, and then, as if he wondered what they were doing there at all, he let her go abruptly. 'Your glasses,' he explained. 'You're not wearing them.'

'Oh. Those grapefruits.' She leaned weakly against the wall, her soft brown hair falling in a cloud around her face. 'For a minute there you scared me. That particular fruit is usually used to described quite another part of one's anatomy.'

'What?' It was his turn to look confused, and then, as the light eventually dawned, his mouth broke into a broad, unaffected grin.

In nine months, it was the first time Roxane had ever seen him smile, and it changed his face completely, making it younger, less formidable, and quite impossibly attractive.

And all at once her tenuous control snapped. She started to laugh, and once she started, she couldn't stop. She laughed and laughed and laughed, and as her ex-employer stared at her in puzzled indecision, the strain of the last two days caught up with her at last—and the laughter changed to tears.

Through the mist in front of her eyes she could see him staring at her, his dark eyes clouded with exasperated concern and his full lips pulled into a strange, twisted grimace. And then slowly, as her sobs increased in volume, she saw him move towards her—and suddenly it was all too much. He held out a tentative hand, his eyes still dark and puzzled, not knowing what to do—and the next moment, she never knew quite how, she found herself clasped firmly in his arms with her face buried against his shoulder, as great, tearing sobs shuddered uncontrollably up and down her body.

It seemed a long time later when she finally lifted her head, which rested just below his chin, and raised her eyes cautiously to his face. His hand was stroking her shoulder and the deep black eyes were fixed on her with an expression she could not interpret. His lips looked gentler somehow, the hardness washed away, but they were still beautifully firm—and tender . . .

She couldn't take her eyes off them.

As she went on staring, and before she knew what was happening, his head had bent towards her and his mouth was pressed softly against her forehead, moving across her cheek to brush the tip of her nose. And then those glorious lips were on hers. As all rational thought vanished in a wave of overwhelming sensation, her one conscious thought was that they felt and tasted just as wonderful as she had known they would . . .

Her arms crept around his shoulders and she wound her fingers through the dark, curly hair at his neck. His kiss was tender, but controlled and very sweet, as if it were meant to comfort more than to arouse. As confusing emotions and wild, unexpected feeling swirled through Roxane's body, he pulled her closer, and her hands moved eagerly across his back, feeling the strong muscles beneath the jacket of his suit. Her lips parted beneath his and she pressed her breasts against his chest, wanting more, more—more than comfort . . .

She no longer knew what she wanted, only that this man was stirring needs and hungers in her that she had never known existed.

His tongue moved between her lips and there was a taste of salt in her mouth—and then, abruptly and unbearably, he had released her and was holding her at arm's length.

'Your lips taste of tears,' he said huskily. The velvet eyes were filled with an emotion she couldn't understand. He passed a hand across his forehead and she was struck again by the fluidity of his movements—like a beautiful jungle cat. Then, as her breathing slowed, and sanity began to return, she remembered that this was no pussycat, jungle or otherwise. It was only hours earlier that she had been calling him a snake.

She put her hand in the pocket of her peach-coloured slacks, searching for a tissue. There wasn't one.

'Here,' he said, moving towards her. 'Use mine.'

Cautiously Roxane took the bleached white square he offered her and wiped it across her face. It smelled clean and nice and, very faintly, of him.

'Why were you crying?' he asked, his eyes still curiously bemused.

'I don't know. Just too much emotion these last couple of days, I suppose. And then you practically breaking down my door . . .' She blew her nose and handed the sodden ball back to him.

He eyed it doubtfully.

'Oh. Oh, I'm sorry,' she muttered. 'Your jacket's all wet, too.' Hastily she removed the handkerchief from his hand and began to dab uselessly at his lapel.

He backed quickly away. 'It's OK. I can get it cleaned.' Gradually the bemused expression faded from his eyes and he added, with a rueful grin, 'You know, this is *not* what I came here for.'

'I know,' she replied in a small voice. 'You came to wring my pretty neck.'

He laughed. 'Well, not precisely that, although I admit the thought did cross my mind. But the courts take a dim view of that sort of thing.'

'Oh. What *did* you come for, then?'

'To administer a good spanking?' he suggested, raising a maliciously challenging eyebrow. 'I don't like being hung up on.'

Roxane eyed his firm thighs and large hands warily and said, with more conviction than she felt, 'The courts take a dim view of *that* sort of thing, too.'

'Pity.' He was leaning against the wall now, his hands in his pockets, and his handsome head thrown back to reveal the tough sinews of his neck. There was a disturbingly provocative gleam in his much-too-attractive black eyes.

Roxane took a deep breath. 'Mr Mardon . . .' she began.

'Yes, Roxane.' His face sobered immediately, and he inclined his head towards her with mocking attentiveness.

She gaped. 'How do you know my name? I thought I was Miss Peters.'

'From the employee records file. And I think we're past the "Miss Peters" stage, don't you?'

'Well—I suppose . . .'

'My name's Gareth.' His gaze still challenged her.

'Oh.' So that was what the 'G' in 'G.M.' stood for.

'And the "M" is for Michael,' he added, seeming to divine her thoughts.

'Oh,' said Roxane again.

'No, not "oh". Gareth.'

Gareth . . . No. Wait a minute. Whatever his name was, it went with Mardon, and it was Mr Mardon who had just wiped out Martha's hopes for a comfortable retirement, deprived Lisa and Art of their livelihood, and inflicted considerable hardship on a great many other good and kindly people. If he thought he could erase all that with one intoxicating kiss—he had almost been dead right. Almost. But not quite.

She drew herself up to her full, slender height and looked him squarely in the eye.

If only he would stop looking like that, so disturbingly male and relaxed, leaning against the wall . . .

'Mr Mardon,' she said firmly, 'this has gone quite far enough.'

'Do you really think so?' The gleam in his eyes was more provocative than ever. Damn it, the man was playing with her.

'Yes—I—do,' she replied, each word separate, distinct—and icy. 'If you came over here to persuade me to give up the interview, you can forget it. I'm not the sort of person who gives up, I can assure you of that.'

He nodded. 'I believe you. Not without a fight, anyway. You gave me some rather damp evidence of that yesterday.'

Roxane fought down an urge to crow. 'Did I? I can't think what you mean.'

She half expected him to exact immediate revenge, but instead this surprising man only laughed.

'Vixen,' he chuckled. 'I didn't deserve it, either.'

That was too much.

'You deserved a lot worse.' Roxane's voice rose indignantly. 'Don't you have any idea what you did to those people yesterday? Don't you even care that jobs are hard to find, and that a lot of them are going to be in real financial trouble? Or that you lied to us, and because of that not one of us will ever be able to trust an employer again?'

He stared at her, a faint frown between his heavy

brows. '*You* won't have trouble finding a job,' he replied with calm conviction.

'No, I don't think I will. But as I just blew all my savings on a holiday in Hawaii, my finances aren't in great shape, either. Anyway, I wasn't talking about myself. I'm young and single and I'll manage. Some of the others won't.'

His frown became almost a scowl. 'Nonsense. They were given lay-off pay. And there's always unemployment insurance.'

Roxane took a deep breath, walked very deliberately across the room and sat down on the couch.

Gareth Mardon watched her from under heavy, lowered lids. After a moment he eased his shoulders from the wall, stalked towards her in a way that reminded her even more forcibly of a jungle cat, and lowered himself, uninvited and much too close, on to the space beside her.

For a long moment he stared at her, eyes set and guarded. Then he reached over and picked up her hand, holding it lightly against his knee.

She closed her eyes.

'Am I really such a monster?' he asked softly.

'Yes,' said Roxane, her eyes still firmly closed.

She sensed, rather than observed his almost imperceptible shrug.

'No one gets through life without some rocky patches. I should know. And I think the Vancouver staff were treated very fairly.'

'How can you say that?' Roxane's eyes snapped open as she snatched her hand away, wincing as her damaged knuckle bent against his palm.

His eyes narrowed slightly. 'Easily. I saw that everyone got what they were entitled to. I can't blow their noses for them too.'

'I know. You saw they got the minimum required by law. And when that runs out, do you really think unemployment insurance is going to be enough for people like Lisa to live on?'

'Lisa? Oh, the woman from marketing, you mean. Pretty girl—with a strong resemblance to a cow.'

Roxane gaped at him. 'A cow? Oh. Because she chews gum, I suppose. She can't help that, she just quit smoking. And apart from the gum, she has three kids, no husband—and now no job.'

'It's not my fault she mislaid her husband. And my employees' personal lives are hardly my concern.' His lips had tightened and he was looking cold and withdrawn again. 'Don't you realise I couldn't move the whole staff to Toronto? Most of them wouldn't want to come, anyway. And whether you believe it or not, this move is essential to the company's future.'

Roxane gave an exasperated sigh. 'Of course I believe it. That's not the point.'

'Oh? What is the point, then?' His scornful gaze raked over her as if she were an ignorant and thoroughly tiresome schoolgirl.

'The *point*,' Roxane ground out through gritted teeth, 'is that you could have given us some notice—*and* more generous lay-off pay.'

'I'm not a gold-mine, Roxane.' His voice was tired now. 'Dart has been sliding downhill for years, and I aim to stop that slide. If I start throwing money around like a fairy godmother, it'll take years to get the company on its feet.'

'Some fairy godmother,' murmured Roxane in a

choked voice.

'All right, Midas in a good mood, then,' he amended impatiently. 'And as for giving you more notice—in my experience people work better when they have some stake in a company's future. Which they haven't once they've been fired. Besides, I still needed you. You would all have taken new jobs the moment you could, and done a bunk—along with as much of Dart's property as wasn't already nailed down.'

Roxane thought of the pens, pencils and Scotch tape sitting in full view on the kitchen counter. But he was wrong. She wouldn't have taken them if Gareth Mardon had played fair.

'Jobs aren't as plentiful as you think,' she said dully. 'And you sure have a jaundiced view of human loyalty, haven't you? Most of us had worked at Dart for years. We had almost a family feeling about the place. We wouldn't have let you down.' She smoothed the crease in her slacks and added slowly, 'Are you really so absorbed in your business, and making money, that you didn't understand that?'

He was staring at her with an expression that was a mixture of irritation and frustration. 'I think you're being very naïve, Roxane. Anything one gets in this world one has to fight for—and then fight some more to hold on to it. There are no free lunches going, and precious little free loyalty. I still feel I handled yesterday the only way I could.'

Roxane shook her head. He was wrong, wrong, wrong, but there was no way she was going to get through to him. For twenty-three years she had always found it easy to trust, and she had rarely been betrayed. People had responded to her openness with equal warmth and trust. But this man's experience must have been vastly different from her own. She wondered what could have happened in his past to make him so cynical and hard. Not that it made any difference. She still intended to make as much public fuss about his actions as she could.

Not for the first time, he seemed to know what she was thinking.

'If you think that newspaper business is going tô happen,' he told her now, 'you couldn't be more mistaken.'

'You think so?' Her brows arched coolly over her amber eyes.

'I know so.' His voice was deep and confident, admitting no possibility of defeat.

'In that case, why did you bother to phone me? And then to come barging in here as if you owned the place.'

The irritated look faded from his eyes and the provocative grin returned. 'Because I was angry and I wanted you to know it. But when you hung up on me I was more than angry, I was flaming bloody mad.'

'So you came over here to get back at me. And just what did you think you could do?'

He grinned again. 'Well, I already made one perfectly practical suggestion.'

'Yes, and we vetoed it.' Roxane was trying desperately not to give way to laughter. This horrible man had a perfectly impossible effect on her—and, watching him now, she saw at once that he was only too well aware of it.

'What *did* happen to the grapefruits?' he asked, his smile growing wider by the minute.

'Nothing. I took them off and put my contacts in.'

'Why wear them at all? You look much younger and prettier without them.'

'That's just it.' In spite of the fact that she thought it was none of his business, Roxane found herself answering his question. 'When I started at Dart I was only nineteen, and young-looking for my age. Mr Foychuk was the personnel manager then, and I wore glasses to the interview because no one ever took me seriously without them. It worked, too. He hired me as his assistant. And I went on wearing the glasses.' She grinned. 'I figured they gave me an intelligent, intellectual air.'

'No,' said Gareth Mardon, shaking his head. 'They give you an owlish, idiotic air.'

'Thanks,' replied Roxane, tossing her soft brown hair and twisting away from him as his hand reached out to touch her. And then, as her bruised ankle hit the coffee-table again, 'Ouch.'

Gareth eyed her quizzically. 'Are you always so hard on yourself?' he asked. 'You have bruises all over your lovely body.'

So he thought she had a lovely body. Was she supposed to feel gratified about that? Of course, the infuriating thing was that she *did* feel gratified—quite ridiculously so.

'Just a couple of scratches,' she said dismissively, determined to ignore the compliment. 'Nina's table has a habit of attacking unwary passers-by.'

Gareth glanced as it sceptically. 'I don't doubt it.' His eyes roamed thoughtfully around the room, and he blinked. 'In fact, I'm amazed your décor hasn't driven you to suicide by now. Does it bite? It looks positively dangerous.'

Roxane laughed sheepishly. 'Sometimes. Most of it's Nina's. She's my room-mate. She says dull colours depress her, but I think she's colour-blind.'

'She must be. And you're either remarkably tolerant or totally insane to put up with it.'

'No, just broke,' she replied. 'If Nina supplies the furniture, I can spend my money on holidays.'

'Oh, yes. Hawaii, you said. Did Nina go, too?' The question was delivered casually, but Roxane had a feeling there was more behind it than idle curiosity.

'No. I went with my boyfriend.' She watched him closely, waiting for the reaction, but there was only the faintest flicker behind his eyes, and she was no wiser than before. For the first time she noticed that there was a thin white scar running from his left eye almost to the tip of his ear. And his nose—it was very slightly crooked, as though it had once encountered a fist—or several fists. What was it he had said about having to fight for what you get . . .? She thought of Michael, who hadn't got what he had fought for in Hawaii. She still resented Michael's calm assumption that, because they were sharing the expenses, he should also share her bed. Hawaii had put an end to that romance in a hurry. Not that she was telling Gareth Mardon that. He could think whatever he pleased.

But looking at his stern, strong profile now, she couldn't tell what he was thinking. And when he turned towards her and she saw the lights deep in his eyes and the soft, seductive smile on his wonderfully virile mouth, she no longer really cared.

'Your boyfriend,' he murmured, in that way that made her stomach curl. 'Is he a serious item?'

'He's not an item at all any more,' said Roxane

unwillingly. She hadn't wanted him to know that. Somehow Michael's invisible presence had been a sort of barrier between her and Gareth Mardon. A safe barrier. Now she felt vulnerable and exposed. But she was not going to lie to him. She couldn't, not after preaching to him about the virtues of trust and loyalty.

His smile was softer and more seductive than ever. 'Not an item,' he said. 'I'm glad.'

'Why?' asked Roxane bluntly, looking him straight in the eye. 'Why should you care? Caring isn't your style.'

'Isn't it?' His dark eyes seemed to turn darker and inwards upon himself. 'You're very sure about that, aren't you? And as for why I *should* care . . .' He shrugged and turned his head away so that she couldn't see his face. 'You're right. There's no reason on earth why I should be interested in the love-life of the deadly Miss Peters.'

'I am not "the deadly Miss Peters",' cried Roxane, rising indignantly to the bait.

'Really?' He turned back to her and his knee brushed her thigh.

Oh, God, she thought helplessly as a tangible shock seared her body, and she saw that his gleaming eyes with the lights in them were very close to her own. Oh, God, this is hopeless. I have to get away from him—now.

But he was looking at her with a very strange expression on his face: penetrating, yet in a way oddly bemused. She started to get up, but his hand shot out and clamped around her wrist.

'Don't move,' he said softly—and she could not have moved if she had tried.

Their eyes met and locked, and she felt his fingers on the back of her neck, stroking very gently. Then his thumb began to explore the soft curve of her cheek, and she gasped.

'What is it?' His voice was low and husky.

'Nothing, I . . . ' Her hand moved tentatively, almost unwillingly, to his chest.

He made a sound in his throat as his knees touched her, and his fingers moved from her neck to run slowly, seductively down her spine. Hypnotically her hands pressed against his chest and smoothed the fine material of his shirt. And all the time his eyes held her— immobile and utterly transfixed. She was drowning in their deep, compelling blackness.

'Gareth . . .' she whispered. 'Gareth.'

His dark head was bent above hers and she could see the thin scar very clearly now. It was throbbing slightly at his temple. Then, with a groan, he had buried his face in the softness of her hair and his lips were against her forehead.

'Gareth . . .' she whispered again.

Now his lips were on her mouth, and he was pressing her back against the mauve cushions of the couch. She could feel the hard strength of his body. Her arms held him close and her hands were in his hair, then inside the collar of his shirt, pushing it back to expose the smooth, tanned skin beneath.

His kiss was hard now, demanding, and his hands were sliding possessively around her waist.

Roxane stifled another gasp. Fleetingly, it crossed her mind that this was all wrong, that Gareth was the enemy, not her lover, and that she must not give in now, to him of all people, when she never had before.

But she had never wanted to before.

And then none of it mattered as she felt Gareth's

hand on her thigh and his tongue searching the tender places of her mouth. His other hand rested on the top button of her sensibly tailored blouse, and he seemed to be waiting for—what? Permission? Roxane shuddered, and tried to pull away. She *must* stop this—now. If she could. But her arms were still around his neck . . .

And then suddenly, incredibly, there was a loud clanking sound outside, and a key turned swiftly in the lock as the door of the apartment flew open with a crash.

'Good grief!' gasped Nina. 'Oh, lord, I'm sorry.'

Her arms were laden with something which looked like a cross between a defective bicycle with wings and a two-headed horse with wheels. It was made of eye-catching crimson and silver metal. As Nina's startled mouth dropped open, her arms went slack. And the whole improbable contraption fell with a clanging crash on to the floor.

# CHAPTER THREE

FOR A moment there was dead silence. Nina, her pretty mouth still open, stared in consternation at the couple frozen like X-rated sculptures on the couch. Then her eyes moved slowly to the crimson and silver mystery at her feet.

'Well, at least it's not broken,' she muttered.

Gareth, still breathing rather fast, heaved himself upright and murmured something about that being unfortunate.

Nina glanced at him suspiciously and turned to look at Roxane, who was tucking her blouse back into her slacks and, in an attempt that was doomed to failure, trying to look unconcerned. But her pink, flushed face betrayed her utterly.

'I'm sorry,' stuttered Nina. 'I seem to have interrupted something. I'll just get this put away, shall I?' She indicated the metal on the floor. 'And then I'll leave you two in peace.'

'No—no, don't do that,' protested Roxane quickly. 'You live here too, and—and—this was all a mistake. Nina, this is—Mr Mardon.'

'Mr Mardon,' exclaimed Nina, bestowing a look of acute disfavour on her friend's erstwhile employer. 'Mr *Mardon?*' She ran her fingers distractedly through her short, blonde curls. 'You don't mean—the *snake?*' Her eyes travelled thoughtfully over the two dishevelled figures on the couch and she added quickly, 'Perhaps I should have said the snake in wolf's clothing.'

'Your room-mate has a charming tongue,' Gareth remarked drily to Roxane. He returned Nina's disapproving look with interest.

'As *you* apparently have a charming way with the workers of the world,' retorted Nina acidly.

'Oh, don't . . .' Roxane held out a pleading hand. 'Don't, Nina.' She passed her arm over her forehead. 'Things—things are quite bad enough already.'

Nina was immediately contrite. 'I'm sorry. And really, I *was* just going out.' Awkwardly she grappled the metal object off the floor and disappeared into her bedroom. Something clanked ominously against a wall, and a moment later she came out again with a denim jacket over her shoulder and a pile of books under one arm.

'I'm just returning these to the library,' she explained, heading briskly for the door. 'I'll be back in about an hour.'

'OK. Thanks, Nina,' murmured Roxane, as the door snapped shut behind her friend.

Gareth's arm fell casually across her shoulders, but Roxane turned her head away and refused to look at him.

Oh, lord, what had she almost done? If Nina hadn't come home at just that moment . . . Roxane shuddered, and Gareth's fingers tightened on her arm.

If Nina hadn't come home, by now she might have given herself to this man. This man who had so cruelly hurt her friends, who used people when it suited him and then tossed them out as if they were of no more consequence than the daily garbage. He didn't even seem to realise what he had done. He thought it was just good business practice.

Business practice—using people. A band clamped suddenly around her heart and her mind went deathly clear. Of course. *That* was why Gareth Mardon had knocked so peremptorily on her door and demanded admittance to her life. She had refused to backtrack on her story to the *Enquirer,* so he had decided to lay seige to her heart. Well—her body mainly, she admitted. He couldn't have expected her to fall in love with him overnight, but experience had undoubtedly taught him that it was a rare woman indeed who didn't fall for his marvellously sexy body—and those intense, wonderfully bedroom eyes.

Gradually she became aware that the eyes in question were fixed with piercing concentration on her profile— or on her right earlobe, to be precise, because her head was bent away from him and she was staring unseeingly at a round black smudge on the purple carpet.

His hand slipped under her chin and he turned her face towards him.

'What's the matter, Roxane?' he asked quietly. 'Surely you're not upset because your colour-blind room-mate with the turpentine tongue happened to find us together?'

'Nina can't help her eyes. And there's nothing wrong with her tongue. No, I'm not upset that she found us. I'm eternally grateful to her for arriving in the nick of time.'

'To save you from a fate worse than death?' His eyebrows rose sardonically. 'Come on, Roxane. I don't go around seducing unwilling victims. But to tell the truth, you seemed remarkably willing. Enthusiastic, in fact.'

His hand was still cupping her chin, and he was watching her from under lowered lids. She could have sworn that what she could see of his eyes was alight with a devilish amusement.

'Hormones,' she said disparagingly, pushing his hand away. 'Just hormones, that's all it was. And you caught me at a low ebb.'

'Seemed like a pretty high ebb to me.' He rested his hand on her knee, and she pushed that away too. He sighed resignedly. 'What is it, Roxane?'

'Nothing. I've come to my senses, that's all. I'm not a complete fool, you know, and I do know that the president of Dart Express is not going to make love to an ex-personnel assistant he has never even noticed before—unless he has something to gain from it. Such as the cancellation of an unwelcome interview with the Press.'

Gareth stared at her through narrowed eyes. Then with an exclamation of impatience he sprang to his feet, pulling her up beside him.

'Don't be absurd,' he snapped. 'Do you really think I need to make my business deals in bed?'

'Probably not. But I suppose it's as pleasant a way as any. That way you kill two birds with one stone. A cancelled interview on the one hand—and a nice bit of crumpet on the other.'

'Some crumpet,' said Gareth bitterly, turning to pick up his jacket which lay rumpled on the arm of the couch. 'But if that's your opinion of me, I suppose there's no more to be said.' He made for the door, but when he reached it, he paused with his hand on the doorknob.

Slowly he turned around, walked deliberately back

towards her and, taking her firmly by the shoulders, pulled her hard against him. This time his kiss was not warm and comforting, but harsh, almost fierce, meant to hurt—and it was over very quickly. The next moment he was at the door again.

'You can forget about that interview, Miss Peters,' he flung back over his shoulder. 'Contrary to that delightful opinion you have of me, I *don't* have to seduce gullible virgins in order to get what I want.'

Roxane was still staring at the door as it thudded closed behind him. She ran her fingers disbelievingly over her tender lips.

When Nina returned home a short time later, she found Roxane sitting on the white plastic chair, her amber eyes very wide and her mouth stretched tight in a grimace of such concentrated fury that Nina almost slipped out again.

But Roxane raised her eyes and managed to croak, 'Hi,' so Nina closed the door behind her and stepped inside the room.

'What's the matter?' she asked.

'Nothing.' Roxane remembered she had had this conversation earlier, with someone quite different, and added disgustedly, 'He called me a gullible virgin.'

'Oh,' said Nina. 'And are you?'

'Am I what? Gullible or a virgin?'

Nina giggled. 'Well, I know you're not usually especially gullible. And as far as I know you were a virgin when I left you this morning, but . . .'

Roxane's compressed lips broke into a reluctant grin. 'Oh, Nina. What would I do without you? Yes, of courst I'm still a virgin. If you think I'd let that odious, arrogant, impossible man make love to me . . .'

'But he *was* making love to you,' objected Nina. 'I saw him. Or was that a rape scene I so thoughtlessly interrupted?'

Roxane gave an exasperated sigh. 'You know it wasn't. Oh, Nina.'

'You said that already,' replied Nina, sinking on to the floor and locking both arms around her knees. 'Oh, Nina, what?'

'Oh, Nina, I could murder that man. With my bare hands.'

'Huh,' said Nina dubiously. 'From what I saw, murder was not what your bare hands had in mind at all.'

Roxane gazed at her gloomily. 'I know,' she admitted. 'That's just the trouble.'

'What is?'

'He's horribly attractive. But he really is an absolute snake.'

'Wolf,' corrected Nina.

'All right, wolf, then.' She shrugged. 'Not that it matters. I'll see him at the interview with the paper, I suppose, and that will be the end of that.'

But it wasn't quite the end of that, because when Roxane phoned the *Enquirer* the next afternoon to discuss the arrangements for the interview, she was informed that they had changed their minds entirely and no longer felt her story would be of interest to their readers. Particularly as Gareth Mardon had left town for Toronto and would be unavailable to comment.

Roxane swore quietly to herself and hung up the telephone. He had said the interview would not take place, and that he didn't need to make business deals in bed. Apparently he had been right. Bastard. She swore again. But at least she would not have to face him, to see those mocking black eyes laughing at her because he had spoiled her revenge. She ought to be glad of that.

But infuriatingly, and typically, it seemed, where Gareth Mardon was concerned, she found that she wasn't glad at all.

The next day Roxane had two job interviews, arranged for her by the unemployment office. The first was with a group of chartered accountants who spoke to her politely and looked very solid and sensible in business suits and ties. When it transpired that they expected her to have at least some idea about which way to hold a cash sheet, she knew she hadn't got the job. Nor did her muttered explanation that she rarely had any cash to enter on a sheet appear to endear her to the manager.

Her second interview was with a Mr Ryerson who owned a boarding kennel for cats while running a mail-order book business on the side. At first Roxane had been a bit suspicious when she heard about the books, suspecting they were the sort which wouldn't pass through Customs. But it turned out they were mostly sober historical treatises on the less publicised aspects of warfare, or journals relating to the care and feeding of cats.

It was a grey, cold day when she pulled her car into the gravelled car park of Ryerson Kennels, but Mr Ryerson greeted her in his shirtsleeves. He was a large, beefy man who wandered out of the first of three long, barn-like buildings looking harried—and he kept wiping his forehead with a none-too-clean handkerchief which, as far as Roxane could see, only served to move the grime around.

'Thank God you've come. When can you start?' he exclaimed, on being informed that yes, she could type if necessary, knew how to pack books, liked dealing with the pet-owning public and, above all, would answer the telephone.

'Damn thing drives me crazy,' he grumbled, running his fingers through his thick, greying hair, and waving her ahead of him into a small, cluttered office liberally sprinkled with fur. 'My wife used to do all that, but she's taken a job in a cheese factory. Says cheese doesn't meow or scratch. Then I had a boy in, but he walked out on me yesterday. Said he didn't like cats. Do *you* like cats?' He shot Roxane a quick, anxious look.

'Oh, yes. Yes, I do,' she replied faintly.

'Good. Can you start right away?'

'Tomorrow,' she said firmly, casting a resigned eye over her cream-coloured interview suit which was now dusted with an interesting collection of ginger and black hairs whose origin was not in much doubt.

When she came in tomorrow it would be a matter of sensible dark slacks and a multi-coloured sweater which wouldn't show accumulated fuzz.

Wondering what she had got herself into, Roxane returned to the apartment. If the new job turned out to be a disaster—as it showed every indication of doing—she would have Gareth Mardon to thank for that too. But beggars couldn't be choosers, and although she wasn't yet a beggar, she soon would be if she didn't find employment. So—the Ryerson Kennels it must be. And whatever else her new job was or wasn't, it would surely be a change from Dart.

Dart. It still seemed strange not to be getting up every morning, rushing through tea and toast, scraping frost off the windows of her little Honda and arriving breathless but just in time at the office—usually to find Annette seated behind her desk having a leisurely cup of coffee and keeping a hopeful eye on the clock. In the nine months Roxane had worked for the personnel manager, Annette had never quite succeeded in faulting her for being late. Last in to work, frequently, but never exactly late.

From Annette, Roxane's thoughts slid back to Gareth Mardon. No. She didn't want to think about *him* ever again. She searched the small living-room for something to take her mind of her ex-employer—and her eyes fell on a new decoration hanging on the wall. The crimson and silver nightmare which Nina had bought yesterday after falling victim to a garage sale on her way home from work.

Roxane sighed. The thing looked positively malevolent, hanging there over a bookcase stuffed with gothic novels, and appearing to fix her with a baleful, metallic eye. But certainly it was riveting enough to take one's mind off anything else. She remembered Gareth's reaction to it and the muttered word 'unfortunate' which had so infuriated Nina. She smiled, feeling guiltily disloyal to her friend. But all the same, Gareth had been right. It *was* unfortunte that the thing had survived the crash.

Gareth. She was back in that groove again.

With another exasperated sigh, she jumped to her feet and stamped into the kitchen to start supper.

When Nina came home later that evening, Roxane noticed immediately that she looked uncomfortable—as if she had just done, or was about to do, something reprehensible.

'What's the matter?' she asked. 'I've got a job by the way, so you needn't worry about the rent.'

'Oh, I'm glad,' said Nina quickly, looking more uncomfortable then ever. 'But it's not that.'

'What is it, then?'

'Well, you see, Jack and I—that is—oh, dear. Jack-and-I-want-to-live-together.' She finally brought it out in a sentence which sounded like one very long, strung-out word.

'Oh, is *that* all?' Roxane laughed. 'Don't look so tragic about it, Nina. I know it's not married, but if it's what you want . . .'

'It is what I want. Until we decide we're ready to get married, anyway. But—well, really I was worrying about you. I can move out, but you'd have to manage the rent all by yourself, and I know your finances are—are . . .'

'In their usual state of chaos,' finished Roxane breezily. 'But as a matter of fact, you see, I've just got this new job, and it's way down Westminster Highway. So if you want to keep on this place with Jack, actually I'll be much better off somewhere closer to my work.'

Nina's face broke into an enormously relieved smile, and she gave her friend a quick hug. 'Thanks, Roxie,' she glowed. 'You're a real prize.'

Roxane didn't feel much like a prize when she started hunting for an apartment after work the following day.

Inevitably she was covered in cat fur, and with the slightly smudged and weary look of someone who has just completed an exhausting first day on the job, her youthful appearance and windswept hair did not seem to inspire much confidence in prospective landlords.

The next day she restored her heavy glasses to their

rightful place on her nose, and immediately afterwards secured a neat, one-person apartment with sliding dors leading to a sunny balcony off the living-room. It was in a small block only a few minutes' walk from the Ryerson Kennels.

She spent the next two weeks getting conditioned to cat hair and cat owners, and organising her imminent departure from the world of purple carpets. Packing and planning and deciding what to leave behind took up most of her time and prevented her from thinking much about her old job—or about Gareth. She also had to decide what furniture she would need in her new quarters. In any case it was going to be pretty sparse at first, because she wanted to build up her resources before making any major purchases. She already had her big double waterbed, acquired in a moment of madness when she had first met Michael, and all she really needed was a table and a couple of chairs. Luckily the apartment came with carpets. Pale gold, she was relieved to note. Not purple. Nina offered her a selection of pea-green and black cushions, but these Roxane declined with hasty thanks.

On the last Saturday in January, which was unseasonably bright and sunny, Jack borrowed a truck and several husky friends and helped Roxane move into her new home.

About half-way through the afternoon, when the major portion of the job was done and Roxane and her helpers were relaxing over beer and pizza, she suddenly remembered the three boxes of books, mementoes and superfluous shoes which she had left behind in the attic.

'It's all right,' said Jack. 'Nina and I have to meet friends for dinner soon. We'll bring your boxes down for you and you can drive over in the Honda to pick them up.'

A short time later Roxane changed from dirty jeans into clean white slacks and drove over to her old apartment. The boxes were sitting on the pavement, and Jack and Nina immediately tried to load them in for her. But it became apparent at once that there was no way the large, unwieldy cardboard crates had a hope of fitting within the miniature proportions of the Honda.

'Oh, dear,' sighed Nina. 'Now what? Jack and I really ought to leave soon . . .'

'No problem,' said Roxane bracingly, jumping out of the car. 'Just let me borrow your suitcases, Nina. They're flat and stackable, so I'll just load all my stuff into them and bring them back to you tomorrow.'

'Sure, but will it all fit?' asked Nina doubtfuly.

'Of course it will,' said Roxane with airy confidence.

'OK, then we'd better get these boxes back inside.'

'No, don't bother. Just bring the cases down. I'll pack them out here. It's much too nice to be inside anyway.'

Nina laughed. 'You're crazy. But if that's what you want . . .'

A few minutes later Jack and Nina drove off down the street, and Roxane was left standing on the pavement surrounded by four large, flat suitcases and three awkward cardboard boxes.

She took a deep breath. Nina could think she was crazy if she liked, but it felt good to be outside for the first time in ages, on a beautiful, warm day with the scent of springtime in the air. She leaned against the trunk of a large sumac tree, staring up through the bare, twisted branches at the sky. Soon its tiny buds would unfurl into a bright blaze of green. In the garden across the road, snowdrops swayed daintily in a soft breath of wind. Roxane smiled. She could stay here for ever, just breathing and dreaming . . .

No, hang on. That wouldn't do at all. She had work to do. Specifically, the repacking of her books and whatever else was in those three intimidating boxes.

'Right,' she murmured to herself, hauling Nina's suitcase on to a patch of low-lying shrubbery in front of the apartment block. 'Books first.'

She tore open the nearest box, and reaching into it found that it contained a lot more than books. Cups, chipped saucers, a set of knives, and two very brief bikinis wrapped in ancient beach-towels followed each other on to the shrubbery in quick succession. There was even a small bedside lamp with a frilly pink shade which her grandmother had insisted she take with her when she left Winnipeg. Nina too had balked at that, and it had been relegated to the attic along with everything else they had had no use for. Oh, dear. This re-packing job was going to prove more of a challenge than she had expected.

A family, consisting of mother, father, a dog and two children, ambled around the corner, saw the activity on the pavement and moved pointedly across the road. They were followed by a couple with their arms around each other's waists, who stepped carefully into the street and pretended they hadn't seen Roxane and her debris.

But when a man in a low white sedan pulled up outside the apartment, and was confronted by a vision of a girl in a pair of red high heels beneath very long legs topped by a neat, white bottom which was bent temptingly towards him, he let out a slow, appreciative whistle.

For some reason, this unlikely apparition in the shrubbery appeared to be intent on stowing what looked like the remnants of a fire sale into suitcases.

'Very nice too, Miss Peters,' remarked Gareth Mardon approvingly, poking his head through the window of the car and continuing to admire the scenery. 'Any special reason for this delectable demonstration? I presume we're invited to view?'

# CHAPTER FOUR

ROXANE leaped up as if she had been stung by a hornet on the part of her anatomy that Gareth was admiring.

'No, you are not!' she yelped, clasping her hands tightly behind her back and facing him with her small nose high in the air and her chin tilted aggressively. Then she added more calmly, 'What are you doing here, anyway? I thought you were in Toronto.'

Gareth raised his eyebrows. 'From that gracious reception, I gather I'm about as welcome as snow at a picnic. Is that what you're having, by the way?' He gestured at the cluttered pavement. 'It doesn't look very edible.' His eyes strayed to the black bikini top which had somehow hooked itself on to her belt. 'Is that the latest in accessories? Charming in the right place, of course. Definitely edible, but . . .' He lifted his shoulders and smiled disarmingly, showing all his gleaming white teeth.

'Oh, shut up,' snapped Roxane crossly. 'It's none of your business, anyway.'

'I suppose not. At least . . .' His smile faded and a shadow crossed his rugged face. 'You haven't been thrown out of your apartment, have you?'

'Would you care if I had?' She had her hands on her hips now and was glaring at him in a way that reminded him of a hissing goose defending her young. Only those weren't goslings on the concrete behind her, but a remarkable collection of items most of which looked as though

59

they should have been relegated to the garbage years ago.

'As a matter of fact, I would care.' He answered her question in the firm, deep voice that she had been trying so hard to forget. As usual, it sent quivers down her spine.

And she believed him.

'Why?' she asked, still belligerent. '*Why* do you care?'

'Don't you want me to?'

Roxane didn't answer. Instead she knelt down and, with furious concentration, began to stuff books, cups, towels and bikinis into the nearest suitcase. Damn the man. Why did he have to come back? Now of all times, when she was in this ridiculous position on the street. And why did he have to look like that? He was devastating enough in his dark suit, but dressed casually as he was today, in a turtleneck sweater which stretched across his wide chest like sinuous black skin, and those clinging black jeans which moulded his tight thighs to perfection, he was almost irresistible.

She jammed two heavy books on top of the bikinis, threw in the frilly lampshade and tried to slam down the lid.

'Here, let me help.' Gareth sank down beside her and rocked back on his heels. He was so close that she could feel his warm man's breath on her neck. She gulped, and drew in her own.

'Look,' he said patiently, 'that's not the way to pack. I should know. I've been doing a lot of it lately.'

Without giving her time to argue, he pulled all Roxane's possessions from the case she had started on, and threw them on top of the shrubbery. Then with deft, efficient hands he loaded in first books, then crockery wrapped in towels so that it nested neatly, and finally a selection of odds and ends whose reason for existence was quite beyond him.

When he came to the black bikini, his dark eyes glinted wickedly and he shot Roxane a look of teasing provocation. She had been glancing sideways at his profile, but she turned away the moment she saw the look, and Gareth, with a mocking, deliberate smile, put a pair of teacups carefully in the top of the bikini and laid it across the towels so that its black sheen gleamed up in the sunlight like two dormant volcanic peaks.

Roxane clamped her mouth shut in irritation, found it wouldn't stay that way, and started to laugh instead.

'That's better,' said Gareth complacently. 'You're much prettier when you laugh.'

She stopped laughing immediately. 'And you're much nicer when you're not smug.'

'Ah. So there does exist the possibility that I'm nice.'

'No, there doesn't. It was a slip of the tongue.'

Gareth's lips quirked and he raised his eyes to follow the gently waving branches of the trees. 'Well, you warned me you didn't give up easily. How long do you propose to keep up this hate you have going for me?'

His hand touched her cheek very lightly, making her flesh tingle, and she sprang hastily to her feet. 'Hate's much too emotional a word. I just don't like you, Mr Mardon.'

He stood up slowly, his long, uncoiling body reminding Roxane even more forcibly of a big, sinuous cat. 'Because you've lost your apartment?' he asked. 'Can't you afford the rent?'

She was surprised to note what looked like real concern on his face.

'No, *not* because I can't afford the rent. Don't flatter yourself, Mr Mardon. You haven't ruined my life. I've found an excellent job and I'm moving closer to my work, if that's what you want to know.'

'I told you you'd find another job.' He was looking smug again.

'Yes, well, I didn't need you to tell me that. But others are not so fortunate.'

'No? Have you heard from others, then?' His voice was quite, dispassionate, but still not without concern. Roxane was puzzled.

'Yes, I have. Martha's still in shock, Art's wife is back in the hospital and Lisa—Lisa is getting desperate—and she's started smoking again, which is the last thing she can afford.'

He nodded, his eyes staring off into the distance—almost as if he hadn't heard her. Then he seemed to shake himself, and, running a hand through his waving black hair so that he looked younger and somehow more vulnerable, he gave Roxane a quick, mischievous grin and said they had better finish packing.

Ignoring her protests, he proceeded to stow all her belongings quickly and expertly into Nina's cases. A few minutes later the cardboard crates were back in the basement of the apartment block and Gareth was loading the suitcases into the white sedan.

'Hey,' cried Roxane. 'Don't do that. I can take them in my own car.'

'No, you can't. They won't fit.'

'Of course they will.' Angrily she pulled the embattled cases from the trunk and began to stuff them into the Honda. The first two packed away with no problem at all. The third was a tight squeeze. The fourth resisted all attempts to cram it into a space two inches high by one foot wide.

Gareth leaned against a nearby beech tree with his arms folded across his chest and his ankles casually crossed. When Roxane finally gave up with an exclamation of disgust, and turned around to face him, he was watching her with a small, irritating smile curling about his lips.

'Don't you dare say I told you so,' she snapped.

'I wouldn't dream of it.' He eased himself away from the tree, his smile more irritating than ever, and, calmly taking the case from her now unresisting fingers, threw it easily into the back of his car.

'I'd better take one of the other ones too,' he remarked, with maddening common sense. 'You won't be able to see through your rear window otherwise.'

Roxane opened her mouth to argue, saw him looking at her with that infuriating grin, and changed her mind. He was right. And he would think she was even more of a fool than he did already if she wrapped herself around a lamppost at the nearest corner.

'All right,' she agreed ungraciously. 'But you don't *have* to help, you know.'

'You've made that abundantly clear,' he replied drily. 'So can we please bring this ridiculous pavement show to an end? I'm sure the neighbours are enjoying it enormously, but in case you haven't noticed, the sun is fast disappearing, you're wearing a rather thin, though very attractive blouse—and really it's time to ring the curtain down.'

Roxane was about to tell him what she thought of his high-handedness, then thought better of it, and with her head held high she opened the door of the Honda to step with dignified silence behind the wheel.

Unfortunately there was nothing very dignified about hitting her head on the roof because she was too busy being superior to look where she was going. Seeing the laughter in Gareth's eyes, and his totally unsuccessful attempt to control the grin on his lips, she was attempted to throw her car keys at his head. But instead she gave him her new address in a cool, disinterested voice, and started up the engine of the car.

At the back of her mind was the awareness that if Gareth deliberately absconded with Nina's cases, it would probably be all her own fault. He really had tried to be helpful this time—and how could she honestly blame him for laughing at the ridiculous picture she must have presented standing at the edge of the road packing a suitcase on top of a patch of shrubbery? Why on earth had she done it? It had seemed a good idea at the time. But then, at the time, she had not expected Gareth Mardon to show up.

Gareth. Why did he always do this to her? With a little snort of annoyance, she pressed her foot on the accelerator—and arrived at her new home a full two minutes ahead of her tormentor.

'You drive too fast,' he informed her, as he carried her cases up the stairs.

'Only when you're around,' she retorted, sitting down heavily on one of the two kitchen chairs which made up the seating capacity of her living-room.

He raised his eyebrows. 'My God. Is there no end to my iniquities?' He sounded weary. 'Where do you want me to put these?'

'On the bed,' she replied, indicating the open bedroom door.

A moment later she heard Nina's property thud down, and Gareth returned to the living-room, wiping his forehead with the back of his hand.

'You must have the accumulation of a lifetime in those bags,' he remarked. 'And you have a waterbed, I see.' He grinned suggestively.

Roxane ignored the last part of his comment and said frostily that he ought to know what she had in the cases, seeing that he had packed them.

'Yes, and I haven't received any thanks yet,' he reminded her.

'Thank you,' she said coldly.

'Mm. Delivered with heart-warming conviction. Tell me, do you always drive like a maniac—and do your packing in the street?'

'I told you. Only when you're around.'

'You pack in the street because I'm around?' Roxane saw the smiling disbelief in his eyes, decided he must now consider her totally insane, and to her complete surprise found that she was smiling back.

'No,' she explained. 'It's true I was speeding because you made me angry—but it was pure chance you caught me packing in the street. It was the sun, you see. We haven't had much this year and I wanted to enjoy it.'

He nodded sympathetically. 'Yes, I think I do see. you're a creature of impulse, aren't you?'

From the reminiscent glint in his eye, she knew he was remembering the water episode.

'I suppose I am sometimes,' she admitted. And then, quickly changing the subject, 'What are you doing back here? I thought you were in Toronto.'

'So you said. And I was. But the Vancouver despatch office is still in operation, you know, so I'm back clearing up odds and ends. In my job you don't find yourself in the same place for long.'

No, thought Roxane, and with your temperament you

can't keep still for long.

'I see,' she said, staring disapprovingly at a patch on the wall where the plaster had been chipped off. But in the same instant it occurred to her that she didn't see at all. He might be in Vancouver for entirely legitimate reasons, but that didn't explain what he had been doing driving down her old street.

She looked up to find him leaning against the wall watching her, with his hands in the pockets of his jeans and looking quite hopelessly attractive. How on earth could she phrase the question she felt she had to ask?

'Umm . . .' she began hesitantly.

'Yes?' His dark eyes opened very wide, as if he expected her to ask him his opinion on the origins of man—or something equally high-minded.

She sighed. 'What in the world were you doing outside my apartment? Don't tell me it was a coincidence?' There really was no less blatant way to put it.

'All right, I won't. I came to take you out to dinner. And to make you a proposition.'

Roxane's mouth fell open. She started to get up, then found she needed to sit, and thumped down hard on to the wooden chair again.

'Don't look so shocked. I don't mean what you think.' He smiled encouragingly. 'Go on, go and put on your face. I'll tell you about it over food and drink.'

Just at that moment, the thought of food, and particularly of drink, was altogether appealing. She was badly in need of some kind of support. She pushed herself up and started to walk into the bedroom. Then she realised she was letting her least favourite person push her around—again—and she stopped.

'I already have plans,' she told him over her shoulder.

'Then change them.'

The quiet arrogance in his voice made the blood flow furiously to her face. She spun around to face him.

'Of all the conceited, self-satisfied beasts . . .' she began. Then she saw that his mouth was split into a broad, friendly grin, and she stopped abruptly.

'I was only teasing you,' he said placatingly. 'Of course I don't expect you to cancel your arrangements—if you have any. I'd want to wring your neck if you ever tried cancelling on me. *Do* you have plans, Roxane?' His eyes were serious now, probing her face and demanding an honest answer.

'No,' she replied sullenly. 'But I do wish you would rid yourself of that obsession about my neck.'

'Does it make you nervous?' He strolled across the room and came to a halt in front of her.

'No,' she said crossly.

'Really?' He raised his square-tipped fingers and cupped them gently around her throat. His touch was like a jolt of lightning streaking through her body, and with his dark head bent towards her and those smoky, hypnotic eyes boring into her own, she knew that he made her more than merely nervous. His nearness was turning her into a quivering, spineless jelly.

With a monumental effort of will, she lifted her arms, removed his fingers from her neck and stepped away from him. 'All right,' she acknowledged. 'You win. You *do* make me nervous. But not because I think you're homicidal.' She took a deep breath and managed a bleak little smile. 'I'm sure your sense of self-preservation is much too healthy for that.'

He nodded. 'Quite right. Although I have to admit,

you've made me come close to it at times.'

'*I've* made *you* come close to it . . .' Roxane discovered she was speechless.

'Frequently. But never mind that now. You've already said you're not doing anything tonight. Fetch your bag, or your face, or whatever it is you women carry, and let's get moving. I'm hungry.'

So was Roxane, but she still balked at the idea of going out with Gareth. He was, after all, the only person she knew who doubled as a snake—and his effect on her was altogether too unpredictable and disturbing.

'I haven't unpacked any clothes.' She put up a last, weak objection, and it did her no good whatever.

'You don't need any.' As the implication of his words sank in, his face lit up with a slow, sexy grin. But he didn't push the subject, and only added neutrally, 'There's a very good seafood restaurant across the bridge in Richmond. It's quite informal. Your trousers and that slinky black blouse will do very nicely. Besides—look at the way I'm dressed.'

Roxane did, and decided she liked what she saw far too much. If he thought her blouse was slinky, he should consider what his black sweater and jeans did to her libido. But then, perhaps he had considered it. He had mentioned a proposition.

Hastily she turned away and went into the bedroom.

When she opened the door again, Gareth was sitting on one of the wooden chairs with his arms resting on the table. And Roxane had her black spectacles on again.

Gareth looked up. 'Take them off,' he said resignedly, leaning back in his chair.

'Why should I?'

'Because I said so?'

'Huh. That won't get you anywhere,' scoffed Roxane.

'I didn't think it would.' He stood up, took one long stride towards her, and removed the glasses carefully from her nose. 'There. That's much better.'

Roxane blinked. 'No, it isn't. I can't see.'

'I suppose that is a disadvantage.' He started to laugh. 'Look, would you put your contacts in if I told you they make you more beautiful? I know it's much more fun to needle me, but—I'll break these blasted black things if you don't.' There was a note of such exasperated, half-amused pleading in his voice that Roxane found herself smiling. Besides, he had called her beautiful.

'All right,' she agreed. 'I won't be more than an hour.'

Five minutes later she emerged from the bedroom again to find Gareth pacing around the room and glaring disparagingly at all the bare, empty spaces.

'You could use some furniture in here, couldn't you?' he remarked. 'What happened to the mauve and green marvel?'

'I told you. It's Nina's. And I thought you didn't like it.'

'I don't. But—it had its uses.' His eyes moved reminiscently over her body, and Roxane felt the colour begin to flood her cheeks. But when, as usual, she couldn't find anything safe to throw, she tucked her bag securely under her arm and said that if he wanted to eat, then perhaps they had better get going.

He glanced at his watch. 'You're right. Our table should be ready in about ten minutes.'

'You were very sure I'd come, weren't you?' she accused.

'Not entirely. But then I'm not totally devoid of resources, you know. I think I could rustle up a dinner partner without too much trouble.'

I'll bet, thought Roxane sourly, annoyed with herself for resenting his 'resources'.

A few minutes later they were seated across from each other in a small, intimate restaurant with long windows overlooking the Middle Arm of the Fraser River. The lights from the nearby Dinsmore Bridge shimmered across the water and Gareth smiled at her—and Roxane sank back in her low padded chair and found herself smiling too.

Suddenly a look of consternation crossed his face. 'I never thought to ask,' he exclaimed, with comical confusion. 'You do like seafood, don't you?'

It was the first time Roxane had seen him when he was not in complete control of a situation—and for the first time she felt a kind of sympathy towards him.

'I love it,' she assured him, and was disarmed by his sigh of relief.

A waiter brought the glass of white wine she had asked for, and she took a long, grateful sip. It slipped warmingly down her throat, and she gave a sigh of contentment. 'That's better. Now—before I go completely round the bend, will you *please* tell me what this is all about? Last time I saw you, I told you I wouldn't let you use me. And I haven't changed my mind. You stormed out of my apartment as if I'd accused you of holding an orphanage to ransom—and yet here you are, back in my life, and muttering about "propositions". It doesn't make any sense.' She picked up her wine glass carefully by the stem and took another sip.

'I wasn't muttering,' he objected, taking a lusty mouthful of his own Scotch on the rocks. 'I was telling you, quite clearly, that I had a suggestion to make. One that I think may appeal to you.'

Roxane looked at him suspiciously. 'If it's *your* suggestion, I should think that's highly unlikely.'

Gareth's jaw stiffened a fraction, and she saw his hands tighten around his glass. Then he said drily, but with a cutting edge to his voice, 'If that's your attitude, I'm inclined to think you're right. But if you want the truth, Miss Roxane Sour-faced Peters, I came to offer you a job.'

# CHAPTER FIVE

ROXANE gaped at him. 'I'm not being sour-faced,' was her immediate, and quite irrelevant reaction. But she knew perfectly well that she was.

Gareth sighed. 'In that case, I hope I never meet you when you're in a really bad mood,' he remarked rudely. 'That scowl would scare off an army of enraged porcupines.'

'Do porcupines get enraged?' asked Roxane, distracted from her ill-humour.

'How the hell should I know?' He grinned. 'But if they do, you'd scare them off.'

She grinned back, her grouchiness vanquished by his ridiculous allusion to porcupines. 'I guess I might at that,' she agreed. And then, staring down at the gleaming white tablecloth, 'What did you mean about a job? You already fired me. Remember?'

'Yes, I remember.' His face darkened. 'But now something has come up—and I'd like to make amends.'

She lifted her head to find his eyes fixed on her with surprising intensity. '*What* has come up?' she asked.

'Annette has decided to retire.' His strong face was partly shadowed by the dim lighting, but Roxane thought she detected an odd reserve in his voice, and there was something very private about even that part of his face which she could see.

She remembered the rumours that he was having an

affair with Annette, and felt a startling surge of resentment.

'Retire?' she replied coldly, remembering that she had never liked Annette. 'I don't see what that has to do with me. And isn't she about thirty years too young to retire?'

'She has her reasons.' His tone was still guarded. 'And as for what it has to do with you—I was hoping you would take her place.'

'Me!' Roxane's arm jerked upwards, and a drop of wine splashed on to the table as she wondered for one, brief, improbable instant just what 'place' he had in mind. Business or—more personal. Then common sense returned. 'But—I'm not a manager,' she argued. 'I don't have the training. And anyway—well, why should you want *me?*'

'Why not?' His voice was low and persuasive, and for a moment she was almost convinced.

'Because—because, that day at my old apartment . . . I mean . . .'

'What *do* you mean?' he asked quietly.

Roxane squeezed her eyes tight shut, then opened them again. He was still sitting across from her, looking impossibly handsome, and obviously expecting an answer. 'I mean you don't even like me,' she said, when she was finally able to marshall her confused and runaway thoughts.

'What makes you think that?' Now he was seducing her with his eyes.

'Well, you were furious when I spilled the water on you . . .' She paused, took a long breath, and then went on, 'And you were furious because I called the *Enquirer*. And after that you got into a temper when I said you were only . . .' She hesitated. 'Only making love to me to stop me going on with that interview . . .'

'I had every reason to be angry about that.' His features hardened. 'Because it wasn't true. But none of that means I don't like you. As a matter of fact . . .' he smiled ruefully, 'in spite of the fact that you frequently incite me to thoughts of some very satisfactory violence—I find you utterly enchanting.'

For a moment Roxane, looking into those deep, seductive eyes, was lulled into believing him. Then she remembered he had lied to her before, and wondered what he hoped to gain this time.

She was about to ask him just that, when the waiter arrived with their orders, and as soon as she saw food she realised how very hungry she was. Especially as it was her favourite, scallops in wine sauce. Gareth, too, began to tuck away an enormous plate of crab and assorted shellfish with dedicated enthusiasm. She liked a man to have a hearty appetite . . .

In the end it was several minutes before Roxane replied to him, and by then she had had plenty of time to think.

'I still can't believe you weren't trying to manipulate me,' she told him quietly. 'And as for finding me enchanting—I thought you just offered me work as your personnel manager, not—as something else altogether.'

Gareth picked up a crab leg and, with his eyes staring stonily into hers, held it in front of him and cracked it, loudly, deliberately—and very slowly. 'My offer was exactly as I made it,' he said curtly. 'I need a personnel manager. Not a mistress. I'd hardly come all the way out to Vancouver if that was all I wanted.' He snapped a mussel shell with one hand. 'And I resent the accusation that I'm lying.'

Roxane shrugged and swallowed a scallop. 'You may

resent it, but I don't see how you can expect me to think anything else. You've lied to me before, you know.'

'What?' Incredibly, he looked genuinely baffled. 'What are you talking about?'

'Dart,' she said bitterly. 'Don't you remember? I and fifty others worked for you at head office. When the rumours started about the move, we were deliberately told it wouldn't happen. Presumably to give us a false sense of security. And it worked.'

'Oh. Yes, I see.' He wiped his mouth on a napkin, and his fingers strummed tensely on the table. After a while he said softly and with quiet assurance, 'I didn't actually lie to you, you know. Nobody asked me.'

'No. We asked Annette, and she lied for you.'

'I suppose it did seem that way.'

'Is there any other way to see it?'

'Perhaps not.' He stopped strumming abruptly. 'In the end it was my responsibility, wasn't it? But I didn't tell her to lie. She took that on herself.'

'But you didn't try to stop her.' It was a statement, not a question.

'No. I wasn't aware of it until almost the end. I was away in Toronto most of that last month, getting things organised. When I came back, the rumours had already been squelched.'

'And if you had been aware of it? Would you have told the truth?' Roxane held her breath, gripped the arms of her chair very tightly—and wondered why his answer meant so much.

He was staring straight ahead of him now, not seeing her white, anxious face. 'I don't know,' he said quietly, after what seemed a very long time. 'I really don't know, Roxane. Annette was the personnel manager. I've never been very good at managing people—at least, not without ruffling their feathers.' He smiled faintly. 'And at the time I was less concerned with the people I was leaving behind than with the ones I was taking with me to Toronto. I did take as many as I could, you know, but in most cases it just wasn't practical.'

'I suppose it wasn't,' she murmured doubtfully.

'Believe me, it wasn't. But to answer your question, would I have told the truth if I'd been asked point-blank? Maybe. I'm not in the habit of lying. But still—I honestly don't know.' He rubbed his thumb absently over his chin, and smiled regretfully. 'I'm afraid that in spite of your conviction that I have steel and nails where my heart should be, I did approach two management consultants for advice on how best to handle the move. And both of them advised secrecy. It's the way it's usually done, I understand. Keeps things running smoothly till the end, and cuts down on vindictive vandalism.'

Roxane nodded slowly and put down her fork. 'I think I see what you mean. But—Dart was different, you know. Or you should have known. There would have been no vandalism. And everything would have gone smoothly. That office, those people—we were almost like a family.'

He shrugged. 'Perhaps. I told you, I'm not good at handling people.' His eyes became distant again, miles away in some dark place in the past. 'In my experience, if you want something badly enough, you take it. Otherwise you end up being trampled into the gutter. By the same token, innocent heads are sometimes bound to roll. I don't like it. But I have to accept it. And I don't ever aim to be one of those heads again.'

Roxane wondered what had happened to him to make him feel like that. But his expression was so hard and forbidding that she hadn't the courage to ask.

They ate the rest of their meal in a sort of disarmed truce, talking casually of everyday things and, it seemed by mutual agreement, leaving the matter of Gareth's job offer on hold. Roxane was surprised to learn that he was as enthusiastic a skier as she was, and he, in his turn, was amused and delighted to discover that she shared his passion for trains—which he never had time to take—and which he told her that as a child had represented freedom and escape. Escape from what, he didn't say, and it was as close as she got to the mystery of his background.

When they had finished eating, Gareth ordered Grand Marnier, heated and aromatic in a deep crystal glass. As the sweet fumes teased her nostrils, for the first time Roxane began to feel warm and relaxed in Gareth's company, and she gave him a smile which, had she but known it, made him want to take her in his arms and make love to her on the spot, in the middle of the restaurant, surrounded by shells and plates and people.

But he didn't of course, and when they rose from the table he held himself rigidly still and controlled. His sudden silence, combined with the set expression on his face, made him look formidable and rather frightening. As he helped Roxane on with her coat, he stood carefully away from her, barely touching her shoulder.

To her considerable irritation, she realised she was disappointed.

When the white sedan pulled up outside her apartment she turned to Gareth with a bright, insincere smile, thanked him for the evening and his help with the moving, and suggested that as it was getting late perhaps they had better say goodnight.

'Oh, no, you don't,' replied Gareth, relaxing his control

and gripping her firmly by the elbow. 'You and I have some unfinished business to discuss.'

Looking into those deep, compelling eyes and seeing the firm, full lips harden, Roxane discovered that her resistance was crumbling fast. When his hand tightened on her elbow and she felt the shock of his touch flame through her body, she knew that she had lost.

'All right,' she agreed. 'You can come in for just a minute.'

Gareth said nothing, but stood waiting for her to move, so she walked quickly towards the front door and started to fumble through her handbag for her key. Because she suspected he was watching her with that amused little smile playing round his lips, it seemed to take for ever before she finally grasped it, sandwiched between a lipstick and a roll of plastic tape.

'You must have taken your Girl-Guiding very seriously,' he remarked, peering over her shoulder into the cluttered depths of her bag.

'What makes you say that? I never got beyond Brownies.'

'Isn't their motto "Be Prepared"?' He waved his hand at the collection of objects weighing down the bag. 'I mean, I can understand powder, lipstick, tissues, perhaps the odd sweet or credit card. But tape, screwdrivers, paperclips and—is that really a dagger I see before me?'

'No,' said Roxane dampeningly. 'It's my slimline flashlight. In case I can't see the lock.'

'I see,' replied Gareth, in that bantering tone she had come to know so well. 'And are you often in the sort of condition that requires you to see the lock clearly?'

'No, but lately I've often been in the sort of condition that gives me an idea for quite another use for my flashlight.' She pulled it out of her bag and feinted with it at his head.

He laughed, caught it in his hand, and they were both laughing as they climbed the stairs which led to her apartment.

'Well,' said Gareth, as the door closed behind them, 'I suppose there's only one place for us to make ourselves comfortable while we have our talk . . .'

'Yes,' said Roxane firmly. 'Right here at the table.'

'Of course,' he agreed grinning. 'Where else?'

Roxane didn't answer. 'Would you like some coffee?' she asked primly.

'No, thanks. I'm still recovering from our meal.'

'It *was* lovely.' She sat down on the chair across from him and smiled.

He nodded. 'So was the company.'

'Don't flirt,' she said severely. 'It doesn't suit you.'

He sighed. 'No. You're probably right. I haven't had much time to learn that gentle art.'

Sometimes, thought Roxane, there was something surprisingly wistful and boyish about this tough, uncompromising and very virile man. All the same, she was *not* going to succumb to what was probably pure blarney.

'Just as well you haven't,' she told him tartly. 'And stop prevaricating. What did you want to talk to me about?'

He stretched his long legs in front of him, leaned back in the hard chair with his hands behind his head, and smiled companionably. 'Who's prevaricating? I offered you a job earlier, remember? Now I want an answer.'

He looked devastatingly sexy like that. So lazy and relaxed. Yet beneath the careless attitude she sensed there was a tensed spring just waiting to uncoil.

She gulped. 'No,' she said quickly. 'I can't.'

'Why not?'

'I just can't, that's all.'

'Nonsense. As you told me once before, you're young and single. There's nothing to keep you here.'

'Yes, there is. I came out here in the first place so that I could enjoy the snow on the mountains—not shovel it off my driveway every winter. Why should I exchange Winnipeg for Toronto? I might as well have stayed there. Besides . . .' She paused, and turned her head away, unable any longer to endure the penetrating scrutiny of those demanding black eyes. 'Besides, I've never been a manager. I'm not sure I could handle it.'

'I think you could. You care about pepole—as I have very good reason to know.' He smiled wryly. 'And you've worked in personnel for over three years. I never heard any complaints. Annette thinks you could do the job. At least . . .' He hesitated. 'She didn't say you couldn't. And in spite of your——' his lips twitched '—*impulsive* ways, I believe you have your head screwed on straight.' He brought his hands down from behind his head, and locking them in front of him on the table, leaned towards her. 'What do you say?'

'No.'

Gareth unlocked his hands, and a flicker of annoyance crossed his face. 'It has nothing to do with the snow, has it?' His mouth was hard now, and his voice grated. 'You just don't want to work for me, isn't that it?'

Roxane nodded, not looking at him, but staring at the pale-gold carpet. 'Yes. That's it.'

'I see. So I'm still an inhuman monster, am I?'

At that Roxane lifted her head, and replied simply, 'I honestly don't know what you are, Gareth. But no, I can't work for you. I'd feel like a traitor to my friends, and to

Mr Ryerson who has just hired me.'

'That's the only reason?' he snapped, obviously not believing her.

'More or less. But I don't understand why you want me, anyway. You could have offered me a job as personnel assistant in Toronto in the first place—if you thought I was so valuable. But the truth is, you barely knew I existed, much less what I was capable of.'

'I knew you were capable of doing your job, or I assure you, you wouldn't have kept it.' There was a steely glint in his eye now, and Roxane decided this was not the time to point out that he had had no such qualms about Annette's ineffectual performance. She also noticed that he made no reference to her suggestion that his offer could have been made much earlier. Roxane felt suddenly cold. She crossed her arms over her chest and slumped down unhappily in her chair, saying nothing.

'I suppose I'm still in the doghouse because I deprived you of your little revenge,' he muttered savagely, striking his hand on the table.

'What?' Roxane was momentarily bewildered.

'Your day in the limelight with the Press,' he explained sarcastically.

'Oh,' she said dully. 'That. A most impressive display of the Mardon power and influence. It must have made your day. How *did* you put a stop to it?' There was nothing to be gained from this discussion, but curiosity overcome her reluctance to give him the satisfaction of hearing her ask.

'Basically, I told them the truth. That the move had been carefully thought out, the pros and cons weighed so as to cause as little disruption to the business as possible. They're business people, so they understood that. As for the way it was done, I told them I had probably made a mistake in letting my personnel manager make the announcement, but apart from that everyone had been treated as well as possible in the circumstances. After that the paper rather lost interest. Not enough scandal, you see.'

'Is that what you think?' Roxane asked bitterly. 'That giving us minimum lay-off pay and not even offering a reference is just normal business behaviour? Not scandalous in the least?'

For a moment there was a curious, puzzled look in his eyes. Then he shrugged his shoulders, shifted his big body restlessly in the chair and sprang abruptly to his feet.

'All right, Roxane Peters,' he said, placing his fists squarely on the table and leaning over her. 'All right. So I'm a louse, a snake, or whatever else it was your charming room-mate was kind enough to call me . . .'

'A wolf,' muttered Roxane morosely.

He snorted. 'Hah. I've had precious little opportunity to prove that one way or the other. Never mind, my dear, since this is obviously going to be goodbye, let's do the thing properly.'

With startling speed he moved his hands from the table and placed them around her wrists. The next moment he had pulled her unceremoniously from her seat. He was standing so close to her that she could smell the scent of his aftershave, and his chin was just touching her hair. She felt a wave of dizziness that nearly knocked her off her feet, and an almost unbearable urge to put her arms around him. But he was still gripping her wrists and there was no way she could move.

Slowly he bent his dark head and pressed his lips over hers. And the remembered sweetness washed over her again. She gave a soft little moan.

This time his kiss was not meant to hurt. It was long and probing, hard and yet gentle—and after a while he released her wrists and put his arms around her waist, pulling her so close that she could hardly breathe. Not that she wanted to, as his hands moved from her waist to her thighs and down further, stroking and exploring every soft curve of her body, slowly and smoothly, as if he wanted to remember the feel of her for ever.

Roxane, with her wrists no longer imprisoned, gave way to her longings and flung her arms around his neck. She could feel the broad strength of his back beneath her fingers, as his body pressed against hers until it seemed impossible that they should ever be apart.

And then, unbelievably, it was over, and he was holding her away from him, his hands still on her shoulders as his eyes roamed over her body and came to rest darkly on her face.

'Goodbye, Roxane,' he said very softly. 'It's been—an experience.'

She gazed at him, speechless and unable to move, as the door slammed behind him and she heard his feet running down the stairs. Outside a car engine roared to life, and, as she regained the use of her limbs and ran frantically to the window, she heard the squeal of the sedan's tyres as it tore off down the road.

Roxane stood with bent head, her hands gripping the sill. When at last she looked up, she wanted to cry after him, 'Gareth, wait! That's no way to say goodbye.'

But it was much too late, because the car was no longer in sight, and Gareth had gone from her life for good.

# CHAPTER SIX

THE following day, which Roxane had planned to spend organising her belongings into some semblance of neatness and order, passed by in a strange, foggy blur. Every time she started to arrange cups in a cupboard or shoes in a wardrobe, she found her eyes glazing over as her mind went back to the extraordinary events of the previous evening.

At first she was confused by her own reactions to Gareth Mardon, but in the end she came to the conclusion that there was nothing very surprising or unnatural in the fact that she seemed quite unable to resist his physical presence, however much she wanted to. He was an incredibly physical sort of man, and she was a woman no different from any other. But she had met handsome men before, and none had had an effect on her psyche as overwhelming as the one Gareth seemed able to produce just by being in the same room with her.

She ran a duster thoughtfully along a shelf. Of course there *was* more to his appeal than just a beautiful body, she had to admit that. For one thing, he made her laugh. But there was still no question about it.

Gareth was definitely a snake.

Oh, it was possible he had not realised the full implications of what he had done to his employees—but still, when he *had* been made aware of his own lack of compassion, he had done nothing about it. Lisa and others

84

were still out of work, and Martha had lost all hope of an easy retirement.

Roxane shook her head in frustration and discovered she had just put a shoe in the bread box.

Time to call a halt—to make herself a strong cup of coffee, sit down at the table and try to get this whole ridiculous situation into some kind of reasonable perspective.

She plugged in the kettle thoughtfully. Why had Gareth been so furious when she had turned his job offer down? If he had been all that interested in keeping her on his payroll, he could have asked her to move to Toronto in the first place.

It was not until she found herself pouring milk into the sugar bowl that it occurred to her that Annette, about whom Gareth had always been cagey, had probably not wanted Roxane as her assistant in Toronto. They had never liked each other much. And at the time of the move Gareth could not have cared enough to overrule his blonde and 'useful' manager.

Anyway, one thing was for sure. If Gareth Mardon had suddenly undergone a change of heart and wanted to make amends, it was too little and much too late. She had no desire to leave Vancouver and all her friends, she still didn't trust him an inch, and she was much better off without him—or his job.

But when Nina came over in the evening to see how the unpacking was getting on, she found Roxane reclining on her bed with an untouched cup of coffee beside her, and holding a book in her hand which she was obviously not reading because she was staring over it at a totally blank wall. Her eyes were fixed and grim—and suspiciously moist.

'Roxie, what is it?' cried Nina, aghast. 'Are you lonely by yourself? Oh, I'd never have asked you to leave if I'd realised . . .'

Roxane blew her nose. 'Of course you would,' she said firmly. 'Jack certainly didn't want both of us. And anyway, it's not that.'

'What is it, then?'

Roxane told her, in considerable but erratic detail. When she got to the part about Gareth and the suitcases, Nina started to laugh, and by the time the whole sorry tale was finished, Roxane was laughing too. Even Gareth's parting comment that she was an 'experience' didn't seem quite so awful any more, and in the end she and Nina went out together to eat hamburgers at the local transport café. From the windows of the unpretentious little restaurant, they could see the lights of the gondola lift flickering up Grouse Mountain like a starlit pathway to the sky—and Roxane knew all at once that she was going to get over this nonsense about Gareth and Dart, get on with her work for Mr Ryerson and have a wonderful time turning her new apartment into a pleasant, non-purple place to live.

This comfortable resolve lasted until the telephone rang the following evening.

At the time Roxane was lying in the bath removing the effects of a day spent cleaning cat-pens because Mr Ryerson, who usually did it himself, was away on a book-buying spree.

Muttering to herself, she sprang out of the bath dripping hairy water all over the carpet, and stumbled into the small kitchen wearing nothing but a very brief pink hand-towel.

It was Martha, and her voice was almost incoherent with excitement and relief.

'I've had a letter from Dart in Toronto,' she crowed.

'It says the company made a mistake and I'm to be paid in full until I reach retirement age next year. Oh, Roxane, it'll make all the difference in the world to me!'

'Of course it will,' cried Roxane delightedly, sharing her elderly friend's joy. 'I'm so very glad for you.'

Ten minutes later Martha hung up, and Roxane had just replaced the towel with pale pink panties and a bra when the phone rang again. Shivering, she ran to pick it up.

This time it was Lisa with more good news. Her lay-off pay had been increased and she had received a glowing personal reference from Mr Mardon himself.

By the time she had fielded calls from Molly, Art and even Jerry the office boy—she could hear him snapping elastic bands in the background—Roxane was covered in goose-bumps and felt like a block of pale pink ice. But she was filled with thankfulness and relief for her friends. For all of them had received substantial increases in their settlements, and a letter of reference had been given to each one.

It was only after she had put on slacks and a heavy sweater, and swallowed two cups of hot chocolate that she remembered to check her own mail.

Yes, there it was, a letter from Dart, Toronto.

She, too, had been given more money. And there was a reference signed by Mr Mardon. It said she was conscientious, bright and alert, good at public relations, and that Dart was sorry to lose her services. Yes, a personal reference all right. But at the same time as impersonal as a computer.

Well, what else did she expect? She had turned down his job and told him she didn't like him. And now it seemed that, after all, he *had* listened to her. Apparently when he slowed down long enough to consider what he'd done, he had gone out of his way to put things right—and at considerable cost to himself. Those settlements would not come cheaply.

Later, when she was eating a tin of stew because there was nothing else in the house, it occured to Roxane that Gareth had more reason to be impersonal than she had taken in at first.

Dart's letter was postmarked a week and a half ago. That meant he must have thought she had received it long before he had arrived so unexpectedly to help her move. Canada Post had obviously struck again.

No wonder Gareth had looked angry and puzzled when she accused him of not supplying references. But surely he must have realised . . .

Yes. Probably he had, eventually. But because he was Gareth Mardon, arrogant, self-confident and proud, he had been damned if he would stoop to enlighten her. He would rather make her feel like a worm when she found out she had misjudged him.

And feel like a worm she definitely did.

'Mr Ryerson,' shouted Roxane three days later, as she struggled with an ancient typewriter on which she was trying to compose a letter to a cat-food supplier who had overcharged on his bill, 'Mr Ryerson, where did you put last month's invoice from this company?'

'Last month's?' Mr Ryerson removed his head from a carton of books on the history of guerilla warfare and looked vague. 'Last month's? What d'you want that for?'

'To check that there were no charges carried over. Before complaining that they're billing us for more than we owe.'

'Oh. Don't worry about that. Just don't pay 'em. I

never keep last month's garbage. You know, Roxane, this is a grand collection of books I have here, a real find, this lot . . .'

'Yes, but Mr Ryerson, what do you do about taxes if you don't keep your paperwork?' wailed Roxane despairingly.

'Mm? Oh, taxes. Keep *some* of that stuff. Leave it to my accountant. He says the same as you.' His eyes suddenly canny, he added mischievously, 'Never gone to gaol yet.'

Roxane sighed as she watched his head disappear into the carton again. Oh, well, there was nothing for it, she would just have to write the letter and hope it was a genuine overcharge.

She was still sighing as she finished the battle with the typewriter and pulled the paper out.

'Hopeless,' she groaned. 'Absolutely hopeless. Never mind, if Mr Ryerson has survived this long, I suppose I will too.'

'Survived what?' asked a pleasant masculine voice above her head.

Roxane jumped, and looked up to see a tall, thin young man bending over her desk. He had a lean face, longish nose and nice dark eyes beneath sleek, well-brushed hair. Under each arm he carried a large, over-fed cat. The ginger one eyed her balefully and looked ready to attack. The black one was yawning and looked so lacking in energy that she doubted if he would bother to attack a mouse, let alone a receptionist.

'Survive what?' the young man repeated, smiling agreeably.

Roxane smiled back, a slightly weary smile. 'Everything,' she replied, not enlightening him. 'Can I help you, Mr . . .?'

'Rogers. I spoke to Mr Ryerson yesterday and arranged for these two . . .'

'Oh, yes, of course.' Roxane glanced at the booking schedule. 'Pumpkin and Eggplant for a one-week visit. Here, I'll take them.'

She reached out her arms to relieve Mr Rogers of his burdens, and was rewarded by an indignant spit and a well-placed scratch on her palm from Pumpkin.

'Oh, dear,' murmured the cat's owner. 'I'm so sorry . . .' He dumped Pumpkin down on the desk and reached for Roxane's hand. 'Oh, dear, you're bleeding.'

'Never mind, it's not the first time it's happened.'

He smiled uncomfortably. 'You should get hazardous service pay. I really am terribly sorry.'

'Don't . . .' began Roxane. But she was interrupted by a yell from Mr Ryerson as Pumpkin landed with a satisfied screech on top of 'Terror Tactics in Malaya'.

'Get this blasted cat out of here,' shouted Mr Ryerson. 'What the hell do you mean—oh! Morning, James. Didn't know it was you.' He rose stiffly to his feet and held out a hand. 'Don't mean to offend one of my best customers. Young Pumpkin here is growing up. Packs quite a punch, doesn't he?'

'Yes, he does,' agreed James Rogers gloomily. 'Can I help you stow them away—quickly, before he does any more damage?'

A few minutes later all was calm again in the office. Mr Ryerson was back with his books, Roxane had washed and bandaged her scratch, and James Rogers was standing over her desk once more, looking guilty and clearing his throat.

'I'd like to make it up to you.' He smiled diffidently.

'Perhaps I can take you out to dinner some night?'

Roxane was startled. 'I don't know,' she said doubtfully, pushing a lock of brown hair absently behind her ear. 'I mean—aren't you going away? Isn't that why we have Ghengis Khan and his mate in there?' She nodded at the cat-pens.

'No, actually it's not.' James smiled pleasantly. 'My mother and my aunt are in town from Kamloops. They're staying at my house for a week. And Aunt Kath is allergic to cats. That's why I'm such a good customer here.'

'I see; but if you have visitors . . .'

'Oh, they don't come to see *me,* they come to shop.' He laughed. 'How about tonight?'

'Well—all right. Thank you.'

He did seem a nice young man. He wasn't put off by the fact that her make-up had all worn off and that she was, as usual, covered in cat fur. And he had nice eyes, too—not like those other dark eyes, of course . . . She picked up a pencil and jabbed it viciously at her blotter. Right. That was quite enough of that. Gareth's eyes were no longer an issue that was any concern of hers.

She gave James a dazzling smile that left him speechless, and said she would see him at seven.

For some reason she spent the rest of the day feeling vaguely discontented—and she couldn't understand it. James Rogers seemed like just the sort of man her parents would approve of. Polite, friendly and good to his mother. Quite easy to look at too. So why wasn't she anxious to go out with him?

When she got home she faced the question again, knowing it had to be answered. And the answer wasn't difficult to find. She was still brooding about Gareth Mardon. Blast the man, anyway. He was proving harder to forget than she would have dreamed possible a week or so ago.

She wandered into the bedroom and sat down on the edge of the bed. Did part of her inability to get over Gareth lie in the fact that she felt guilty about accusing him of being self-centred and heartless when, as it turned out, he had shown he had at least some heart tucked away in that broad, expansive chest. Yes, perhaps that was it. And if she wrote and acknowledged his letter and the receipt of the extra money—which was something she should have done anyway—maybe she would manage to exorcise him for good.

That had to be it. She hurried back to the living-room and pulled out a pad of paper.

Inevitably the letter took longer than she had anticipated —mostly because she couldn't decide how to sound suitably aloof, while at the same time admitting that she had been at least partially wrong in her estimation of his character.

Eventually she wrote a brief, cool letter apologising for having misjudged him and thanking him for the reference and the money. It seemed to hit almost the right note. But it really was terribly impersonal—like his reference.

In the end she added a postscript saying she had enjoyed their evening together—or most of it—and hoping he was comfortable in Toronto. The temptation to mention that she had read about the blizzard in Ontario and that the crocuses were already up in Vancouver was too strong to resist. So she added that as well.

By the time she had finished, it was almost seven o'clock. James would be here any minute.

She skidded into the bathroom, had a quick shower, blew her hair until it was almost dry and pulled on a soft yellow jersey dress, all in the space of ten minutes. When James rang the bell she was just applying the finishing touches to her lips.

Breathless, glowing with exertion, but as usual not quite late, Roxane threw open the door and gave him a welcoming smile.

You smell so fresh and clean,' he remarked approvingly.

Yes, thought Roxane as they climbed into his car. And just how freshly clean you'll never need to know.

The restaurant James took her to was very different from the small, intimate one she had visited with Gareth, and she was glad of that. La Belle Etoile was perched halfway up a mountain on the North Shore of the city, and one did indeed seem to be dining high in the sky with the stars. Long panes of curving glass looked across the water to the twinkling lights of Vancouver, and a new crescent moon hung just outside the window, as though it had been specially arranged by the management. The room was large and elegant, and black-coated waiters hovered discreetly in the background.

James looked very young and attractive in his dark suit, and it was an evening made for romance. But somehow the chemistry wasn't there.

Roxane made James laugh with her tales of Mr Ryerson and his cats, and James responded eagerly with stories about his own well-upholstered felines. He also told her about his job as a computer salesman, and Roxane knew he must be doing very well at it when he mentioned that he had already managed to buy a comfortable small house near his work.

It was a pleasant evening, and Roxane enjoyed James's company, as he appeared to enjoy hers. In fact, it was

exactly the sort of evening that would almost inevitably
have led to at least a brief romance only a few months ago.

But when James returned her to her door quite early in
the evening, and did not even attempt to kiss her, she was
relieved. She was also surprised that he asked her out
again.

Roxane hesitated. Well, why not? She had no other
plans, and it *had* been a nice enough evening—and James
Rogers was a nice enough man.

It was only later, as she lay tossing restlessly on her bed,
that she was forced to admit that 'nice enough' was no
longer quite good enough. She wanted more than nice, she
wanted exciting, intoxicating, intriguing. In short, she
wanted Gareth Mardon.

'Oh, lord,' she moaned to Nina on the phone the next
day. 'Do you think I'm falling in love with him?'

'Probably,' said Nina, in a voice which sounded frankly
disapproving.

'You mean *this* is what being in love feels like?'

'Well, it sounds an awful lot like it. I'm not you, of
course, but if you can't sleep, can't enjoy an evening with
a man as perfect as your James, and can't think about
anyone else—Roxie, you *are* eating, aren't you?'

'No,' said Roxane grumpily. 'I've just had another can
of beef stew, but you can't call that eating.'

'Oh, that's all right, then,' said Nina, ignoring her
friend's bad temper.

'No, it's not. Nina—do you really think I'm in love?'

'Oh, for heaven's sake!' Nina was exasperated. 'You're
the only one who knows the answer to that one, Roxie.
But—I suppose you easily could be. Though why you
should want to fall for . . .'

'I know. A snake like Gareth. But I'm really not sure he

is a snake any more. And, oh, Nina, I *don't* want to fall in love with him.'

'Then don't,' said Nina unhelpfully. But, realising her friend needed reassurance, not criticism, she added more sympathetically, 'I'm sorry. Of course I know that's easier said than done. And I shouldn't let my own view of Gareth colour my feelings about—about *your* feelings.'

'That's all right,' said Roxane wearily. 'But what do you think I should *do?*'

For a moment there was silence on the other end of the line. Then Nina said quietly, 'I think you should go on seeing James. Or anyone else you fancy. Just don't sit around moping. It won't help, and it won't bring Gareth back—if that's what you actually want.'

'No, no, I don't. Oh, Nina, I don't *know* what I want.'

'You don't have to tell me that,' replied Nina drily. 'Take my advice, Roxie. Go out and enjoy life—and don't leave yourself time to think.'

Roxane did take her friend's advice. She went to a movie with James on Saturday, to a hockey game with him on Wednesday—and, after a leisurely dinner on Friday, he finally tried to kiss her.

They were standing in the panelled hallway of his house and he was just about to take her home after a nightcap in his austere, but stylishly decorated, regency-striped sitting-room. When he put his arm around her waist she started to draw back. But then she thought, what the hell, nothing ventured nothing gained, so let's see what it feels like.

It didn't feel like anything in the end. Just cold, damp lips on hers and the faintly stale smell of his breath. He must have felt the same, because he let her go very quickly, and a short time later they were on their way back to her apartment.

She didn't ask him to come in, and she was surprised that he asked her out again for a week the following Saturday. He said he would be away on a sales trip in the meantime.

Reluctantly, Roxane agreed. She didn't really want to, but Nina was right. It was essential to keep busy.


At precisely seven o'clock on the day arranged, Roxane applied the finishing touches to her make-up and turned towards the door. His knock came right on cue. James was always precisely on cue.

Sighing for no particular reason, she went to let him in.

For one irritating moment the door stuck. Muttering under her breath, she gave it a sharp tug and immediately fell backwards as it swung contrarily open.

'Hey, watch it. There's no need to break your beautiful neck. I've changed my mind about that.'

Roxane gasped as a man's arm grabbed her around the waist and prevented her from crashing inelegantly to the floor.

She looked up slowly, knowing what she would see.

Not James Rogers' amiably smiling face, but the stern, slightly cynical features of Gareth Mardon—the man whom she had almost convinced herself she would never see again.

# CHAPTER SEVEN

FOR a moment Roxane felt as if she had fallen over a precipice, with the ground tumbling in an avalanche all round her. She closed her eyes.

When she opened them again, Gareth's arm was still around her waist, and his unforgettable eyes were fastened on her in something like alarm.

'Are you all right?'

Hearing his voice, she almost swooned again. How could she possibly have forgotten that warm, sexy drawl that made her stomach curl uncontrollably? 'Yes. Yes, I'm fine.' Her own voice was huskier than usual, and she was finding it hard to think, let alone speak coherently.

'Well, you don't look it,' he said roughly. 'You've gone green around the gills. Come on, you'd better sit down.' He glanced quickly around the room. 'Still no furniture, I see. I thought you might have outgrown your camping phase by now.'

He was moving her towards a chair as he spoke, and when they reached it he took her firmly by the shoulders and pushed her down.

Roxane frowned up at him resentfully. Back less than five minutes, and already he was ordering her around and criticising her life-style.

'Nobody asked you to come here,' she replied. 'And if you don't like my furniture, you can leave.' The initial shock of his return was rapidly giving way to a familiar irritation.

'As a matter of fact, it's your *lack* of furniture I object to. But you're quite right. I don't have to stay. Don't you want me to?' There was a challenge in the gleaming black eyes that made Roxane look quickly away.

As usual, he had gone straight to the root of the matter. And the truth was that she *didn't* want him to leave. The moment he had appeared at her door, she had known immediately that he was the one person she wanted to see more than any other. So why was she hesitating?

He was still standing above her, his legs spread apart and his eyes demanding an answer.

Roxane sighed. 'No,' she replied reluctantly.

'No, what?'

'No, I don't want you to go.' If he was trying to make her grovel, then he had succeeded triumphantly.

But there was no triumph in the relieved grin he gave her now, and in a moment he had pulled her to her feet again and was planting a boisterous kiss on her slightly parted lips.

'I didn't think you did,' he said simply.

'Did what?'

'Oh, lord. Are we going to start that all over?' He laughed and kissed her again. 'I didn't think you wanted me to go.'

'No,' agreed Roxane, as a knock came on the door, 'but I'm afraid you'll have to all the same. I'm going out, you see.'

Gareth stepped back, and for the first time took in Roxane's low-cut apple-green dress with the dropped waist and soft pleats falling to just below her knees.

'Yes,' he said. 'I do see. Who's the lucky man?' There

# IT COULD HAPPEN!
## YOU COULD BE A HARLEQUIN MILLIONAIRE!

**THE FUN:** You could win $1,000,000.00 (a lifetime annuity of $25,000.00 a year for up to 40 years!) if your unique Sweepstakes Entry number turns out to be *the winning number* ... or you could win one of 5,040 other cash prizes ... AND if the secret registration numbers under the scratch off on your lucky keys match—you're also in the running for a gleaming new Caddy! But you can't win anything if you don't enter! It's easy and fun, so do it today! (See official rules in the back of this book for details.)

**THE FREE GIFTS:** You could also get 4 FREE Harlequin Presents novels (worth $10.00 retail) to introduce you to the benefits of the Harlequin Reader Service®. You are under no obligation to purchase any more. You may keep the free books and return your statement marked ''cancel.'' The free books are yours to keep no matter what. But we hope that after reading these novels you'll want to see more. So unless we hear from you, every month we'll send you eight additional novels to read and enjoy. If you decide to keep them, you'll pay the low members-only discount price of just $2.24* each—a savings of 26¢ per book! And there's *no* charge for shipping and handling! There are *no* hidden extras!

If you're not fully satisfied you can cancel at any time simply by sending us a note or a shipping statement marked ''cancel,'' or by returning any unopened shipment to us by parcel post at our expense.

**THE EXTRA GIFT!** And, to thank you for accepting the 4 free books, we'll send you a FREE ''mystery'' gift—yours to keep whether or not you subscribe to the *Harlequin Reader Service*.

*In the future, prices and terms may change, but you always have the opportunity to cancel your subscription. Sales taxes applicable in NY and Iowa. All orders subject to approval.
Offer limited to one per household and not valid to current Harlequin Presents subscribers.

was an edge to his voice now, and his eyes were no longer laughing.

'His name's James Rogers. Not that it makes any difference.' Another knock sounded on the door, louder this time. 'And I really must let him in.'

'I don't see why,' Gareth murmured aggravatingly behind her, as she went to open the door.

Roxane lifted her chin and pretended she hadn't heard.

'Hello, James.' She greeted her date with brisk cheerfulness and an assumed smile of welcome. 'How was your sales trip?'

'Very successful, thank you. How have my cats been behaving . . .?' He broke off abruptly as his eyes fell on Gareth, who was leaning easily against the window with one arm stretched along the sill. Roxane thought he looked almost menacing, with his dark form silhouetted against the light from the street and that devilish smile playing at the corner of his mouth.

James must have had the same feeling, because his eyes widened with shock, and when he tried to speak, only a funny croaking sound came out.

The contrast between the two men was startlingly obvious as Roxane stood with a hand on the table for support, looking from one handsome face to the other.

They were both tall and both wearing well-cut business suits, but, compared to Gareth, James looked very young and ineffectual with his mouth slightly open and the colour rising rapidly in his cheeks.

Gareth, on the other hand, looked exactly what he was. Masterful, strong and well in control of the situation.

'Good evening,' he said smoothly. 'My name's Gareth Mardon. Miss Peters' ex-boss. Roxane, are you going to introduce me to Mr . . .' His eyebrows rose enquiringly and, Roxane was sure, in a manner intended to provoke.

She gulped, and then was furious with herself—and with Gareth Mardon too, for no reason she could put her finger on. 'This is James Rogers,' she said quickly. Then added more decisively, 'My date for the evening.' Now it was her amber eyes which challenged Gareth's dark ones.

But he only smiled lazily, somehow managing to look larger than ever as he swung towards the door. Larger and sexier, thought Roxane despairingly, watching the sinuous way his body moved within the confines of his clothes. And he's leaving. Oh, *why* did James have to come tonight?

As Gareth reached the door she took a step towards him. Casually and possessively he turned around, reached a hand behind her neck to pull her face up to his and kissed her, quickly and thoroughly, on the lips.

'Goodbye,' he said lightly when he had finished. 'Enjoy your evening, Roxane.'

Roxane, with her back to James, stared at the closed door. He had done it again. Kissed her as though it was his right, and then offered a casual goodbye. She tightened her lips and squared her shoulders determinedly. This time there was no question of calling after him to wait. She wouldn't give him the satisfaction. And anyway, James was here.

James. She turned back to him with an apologetic smile. He was standing by the table looking sulky and embarrassed and younger than ever.

'I'm sorry if I interrupted something,' he said stiffly, his face an unattractive shade of red.

'Of course you didn't,' she said heartily, years of her mother's training, and her own sensitivity to people's feelings, coming to her rescue. 'Of course you didn't.

Gareth's just—my ex-boss. That's all.'

'Remarkably intimate behaviour for "just an ex-boss",' complained James huffily.

Roxane couldn't argue with him there, and she was not surprised when he brought her home immediately after a rather indifferent meal at an equally indifferent restaurant, and made no suggestion that they should meet again.

So that was the end of James. Not that it mattered. They had been wrong for each other from the first. Just as she and Gareth were wrong for each other.

She wondered if this evening was also the end of Gareth, but had a feeling this time that it was not. That unpredictable man had been zooming in and out of her life like a boomerang on hot bricks ever since Dart had closed down. There was no particular reason to suppose he would change now. Except that this time he had met James.

Roxane took out her contacts, kicked off her shoes and slumped down on the edge of the bed. Did she want him to come back? Deep down, she knew she did. But life was so much more peaceful without him . . .

She closed her eyes, and when she woke up again the sun was streaming through the bedroom window, bathing her face in the light and warming her chilled limbs. She was still wearing her green dress, which was creased and twisted around her legs—and someone was hammering loudly on the door.

'Who is it?' she called, glancing quickly at her watch, which she had neglected to remove from her wrist. It was precisely seven a.m.

'Gareth,' came the forceful reply, as the thundering on the door continued. 'Who the hell did you think it was?'

Who indeed? Who but Gareth Mardon would come pounding on her door at seven o'clock on a Sunday morning when she was fast asleep and still wearing last night's clothes?

'I thought it was the Angel Gabriel announcing the Last Trump,' she called back sarcastically. *Why* did he have to make so much noise? She put a hand to her head. 'Do stop that racket, Gareth. I'm coming.'

The racket stopped immediately and Roxane groped for her glasses and padded across the room to let him in.

'Do you spend your *entire* life trying to exterminate doors?' she asked irritably, as he stepped across the threshold.

He looked startled. 'I don't think so. What makes you say that?'

Roxane shook her head helplessly. The man didn't even know that it was possible to announce his presence without waking up the dead—or at least every other tenant in her apartment block.

'Never mind, it doesn't matter,' she said resignedly. 'Do you realise it's only seven a.m.?'

'Sure I do. I thought you might make me breakfast.' He paused, and eyed her frazzled appearance doubtfully. 'On second thoughts—change of plan. Why don't *I* make breakfast for us both while you take those damned glasses off, have a shower and—repair the ravages of last night?'

Roxane looked at him tiredly, and was surprised to see that he looked as stuffy and disapproving as her grandfather would have done. She smiled inwardly. So the worldly Mr Mardon had old-fashioned ideals, after all.

She smiled sweetly at him. 'That's a lovely idea. Why don't you? There's bacon in the bottom of the fridge and the eggs are in the egg rack. Oh, and you'll find the frying pan in that cupboard.'

Gareth raised an eyebrow. 'Does madam have any further instructions? A little caviar, perhaps?'

Roxane laughed. 'You can save the caviar for later, Jeeves. That will be all for now.'

Gareth growled, and lunged towards her, but she ducked away from him and made a dash for the door of the bathroom. He was too quick for her. Just as she was about to slam it in his face he caught her by the shoulders from behind and spun her around to face him.

'Witch,' he said, laughing into her smiling, upturned face. Then, as their eyes held, his expression changed, became softer, and suddenly he reached up, removed her glasses, and placed them carefully on a built-in shelf above her head. Then his arms were around her waist and his lips were against her cheek, moving inevitably, tantalisingly, towards her mouth.

He kissed her for a long time, slowly and tenderly, and she held him close and returned his kiss with all the ardour of what she now knew, beyond a shadow of doubt, was her newly awakened love.

Then very gently he unclasped her arms and held her away from him. His eyes moved speculatively from her flushed, still sleepy face, to the crumpled apple-green dress and twisted stockings beneath.

'Go on,' he said gently. 'You must have had quite a night. Go and have your shower.' He turned her around and gave her a little shove towards the bathroom.

It was only as Roxane stood under the shower, remembering Gareth's kiss, and letting the warm, soothing water comfort her chilled and aching body, that she realised that all her fresh clothes were in the bedroom.

Help. Now what? She didn't want to put the green dress on again now that she was all clean from the shower. And if she paraded in front of Gareth in a bath towel, it would only confirm his undoubted suspicion that she was the sort of person who had wild and wanton nights with any man who happened to be handy. Still, there was nothing for it.

Wrapping the white towel discreetly around her body, she tucked in a corner and gingerly opened the door.

An intoxicating aroma of coffee and frying bacon met her nostrils. She sniffed appreciatively, and tried to slip into the bedroom unobserved.

Gareth had his back to her as he stood over the stove. He was wearing a white shirt rolled up to the elbows and she could see the muscles in his forearms as he expertly flipped an egg. His dark hair had grown longer since she last saw him and it curled endearingly on his neck. Her eyes travelled down over the tight jeans covering his thighs. Mm. Very nice from the back as well as from the front, was Gareth.

Trying to make a little noise as possible, she slid unobtrusively along the wall. But a flash of white caught Gareth's attention and he swung quickly around. His dark eyes widened as he saw the slim, pinkly gleaming body enfolded quite properly, but very temptingly, in a brief white bath towel.

Slowly he put down the egg-turner. 'Don't do that to me,' he groaned. 'It's unfair treatment of cooks.'

Roxane giggled and darted into the bedroom. 'Keep your mind on the eggs,' she shouted at him through the partly open door.

When she had hastily pulled on brown trousers and a soft beige angora sweater, and fitted her contacts in, she hurried back to the kitchen. Gareth was still leaning over the stove, but now he was muttering, 'Eggs,' under his breath. 'Eggs, she says. How can I keep my mind on eggs, when she goes around dressed like that?'

'I don't go around "dressed like that",' she said briskly behind him. 'I'm perfectly respectable now.'

He turned slowly around. 'So you are,' he said glumly. Then he grinned. 'Or as respectable as you'll ever be.'

Roxane punched him in the chest, and he promptly put down the egg-turner again and swatted her on the behind. By the time she had punched him again and he had responded by kissing her soundly, the eggs were going brown around the edges.

'OK, romantic interlude over,' said Gareth decisively. In a moment he had plates on the table, sizzling bacon on the plates, and on top of the bacon, eggs that had seen better days.

But it didn't seem to matter. They sat at the little table in the almost bare room and Roxane said it was the nicest breakfast she had tasted in her life. She felt happy and domestic—and almost married—with Gareth sitting across from her, eating so purposefully. Although *he* was the one who had been domestic, she thought wryly. *She* had been cavorting about in a bath towel.

When they had both finished, Gareth leaned back in his chair and stretched his long legs easily in front of him. 'Well, Miss Peters,' he said, giving her a slightly acid smile, 'did you enjoy your wild evening with James?'

'It's none of your . . .' began Roxane automatically. Then she saw that he was laughing at her. He *knew* she had not enjoyed it. 'No,' she said frankly, beginning to smile herself. 'I didn't much. And it *wasn't* wild, in spite of my appearance. I was tired and I fell asleep, that's all.' She fixed him with a disapproving eye. 'And you had no business upsetting James like that.'

Gareth grinned. 'I know it wasn't wild,' he said, ignoring the remark about James. 'Because if I'd had a wild night with a beautiful woman, she sure wouldn't have had her clothes on in the morning.' His grin was now pure devilment, and Roxane felt her stomach turn over at the image he was deliberately inspiring.

'You're impossible,' she said inadequately, turning away from the wickedly gleaming eyes.

'Am I?' Something in his voice made her look at him again, and she saw that his eyes weren't teasing any more, but veiled and enigmatic.

'Yes,' she insisted firmly. 'Quite impossible. Gareth . . .?'

'Mm?'

'Did you just come back to say goodbye again?'

'What does *that* mean?'

'It means—you keep turning up, and turning my life upside-down, and then kissing me goodbye very finally—and as soon as I'm used to the idea, you come back—and kiss me goodbye again. I'm tired of your goodbyes, Gareth.'

Her clear amber eyes were fixed on him earnestly. And he looked at her sweet, serious face and knew that he too must speak the truth—or as much of it as he dared at the moment. The whole truth now might frighten her away. Besides, he wasn't at all sure he knew what the real truth was. Gareth Michael Mardon, who had always known his own mind, found he wasn't sure of anything any more.

'I didn't come to say goodbye,' he told her seriously, 'I'm here for a couple of weeks on business. You see, when you turned down that job I was angry. Disappointed, really, I suppose. But then I thought about it, and realised you had every right to refuse a job you didn't want—with a man you didn't like.'

Roxane opened her mouth to object, but he held up his

hand to forestall her. 'And then I got your letter. I decided perhaps you didn't hate me after all—and that next time I was in Vancouver, perhaps I could—repair the damage I'd done. That maybe we could be . . .' He hesitated. 'Friends?'

'I see,' said Roxane drily, wondering what he meant by friends. 'So you arrived on my doorstep like a piece of returned mail and proceeded to upset my date.'

'I did no such thing,' protested Gareth in an aggrieved voice. 'I behaved like a perfect gentlemen and left the field clear for your James.'

'He's not my James. And perfect gentlemen don't kiss people in front of their dates.'

'I'm glad he's not your James. And it was an entirely avuncular kiss,' said Gareth virtuously. 'Besides,' his eyes twinkled disarmingly, 'I was jealous.'

'Avuncular, my eye,' scoffed Roxane. Then she laughed. 'All right, you're here. We're friends. So where do we go from here? Because if you don't have any better idea, I'm going back to bed.'

'Great idea.' He grinned lecherously.

'Alone.'

He sighed. 'I was afraid you'd say that. Did James keep you up late?' he asked mockingly. 'He doesn't look the type.'

'He's not. But I don't think I slept well on top of the bed, and I've got a splitting headache.'

He nodded. 'I'm not surprised. James would give me a headache too. OK, I'll go back to my apartment and call for you at eight. All right?'

'Your apartment? But you live in Toronto.'

'Yes, but I've kept on the apartment here. It's useful when I'm in town.' He had jumped to his feet and sounded impatient now. Roxane wondered if he would ever manage to sit still for any length of time, and came to the conclusion that he wouldn't.

'Yes, all right,' she agreed. 'See you at eight, then.'

By eight o'clock Roxane, for a change, was dressed, completely ready, and standing by the window. Gareth was not going to get another opportunity to assault her door, or she might be thrown out of her new home. She had made a point of setting her alarm so that she had plenty of time to select a blue and green pleated skirt and a soft white lacy blouse that, with luck, would do for whatever Gareth had in mind. Then she had discreetly applied make-up, brushed her brown hair until it fell in a shining sheet below her shoulders, and attached two minute silver ear-rings in the shape of hearts to her ears.

Now as she stared down into the dimly lit street and watched the wind blow the dark, shaggy branches of the evergreens, she wondered if he would come, after all. She looked at her watch. It was ten past eight and he wasn't usually late. But he *had* seemed jealous of James. Had he meant it, or was he just teasing her . . .?

At eight-fifteen the white sedan hurtled round the corner and pulled up at the kerb. Roxane had the door open before his foot was on the bottom step of the stairway to her apartment.

'I'm not *that* late,' he protested, as he saw her standing above him.

'I know, but I didn't want you disturbing the other tenants.'

He laughed. 'Am I that bad?'

'Worse. Come on in.'

Gareth didn't need urging. 'You look good enough to eat,' he told her, his eyes running appreciatively over her slender figure. 'And I apologise. I would have been on time, but something came up.'

'Oh?' Roxane was determined not to show her curiosity. But he was telling her anyway.

'Yes. You see I have a neighbour called Liz. She lives in the apartment next to mine. She's been good to me. Bringing me pies and cookies so I wouldn't waste away.' He grinned. 'She has this laudable notion that men need looking after. Anyway she came over this evening in an awful state because her mother has been rushed to hospital, her husband's away on business—and she couldn't get anyone to look after Toby.'

'Who's Toby? The dog?'

'Lord, no,' said Gareth, throwing back his head and giving a roar of laughter. 'Toby's her very enterprising three-year-old. And I'm afraid he's at my place for the evening. Maybe even the night.'

'Oh,' said Roxane, quite overwhelmed by this totally unexpected aspect of Gareth's personality. She had no difficulty picturing him in the role of relentless businessman or energetic tycoon. But as a *babysitter?* No, really . . .

Gareth misread the expression on her face. 'I'm sorry,' he apologised again. 'I won't be able to take you out for dinner, of course. But if it's all right with you, I can whip up something at my place. I hope you don't mind children.'

'No, no, I love them,' she said faintly, still unable to take in the fact that hard-boiled Mr Mardon apparently didn't mind kids either. She glanced behind him. 'But—where *is* Toby?' That Gareth could mislay his young charge with careless indifference was much more in keeping with her view of his character.

'Mm? Oh, he's at home. The teenager next door is with him till I get back, then she has to go out. Come on.' He seized her hand and started to tow her towards the door.

'Wait!' cried Roxane.

He stopped abruptly, and she cannoned into him. 'What's the matter?' he asked, looking impatient and confused. 'I thought you said you liked kids.'

'I do,' laughed Roxane. 'But I also need my coat. Just hold the rapid transit for a minute.'

Gareth held it for another half a minute, and then they were speeding through the shaded streets to his apartment near English Bay.

They took the elevator to the sixth floor, Gareth put the key in the lock, and soon they were standing in a large, airy room with a dove-grey carpet, velvet-soft black leather sofas, and floor to ceiling bookshelves on three walls. The fourth was a wide, curving pane of glass overlooking the bay. From the corner of her eye Roxane could see the lights of small boats anchored far out in the white-tipped waters.

Then all she saw was the sticky, ecstatic grin of a small boy in yellow pyjamas who was running towards Gareth with his short arms outstretched and his eyes brimming with delighted welcome.

'Gaff,' he shouted, 'Gaff, Gaff, Gaff, you're back.'

Gareth crossed over to the child and squatted down in front of him. 'Hello, Toby,' he said gently, in a tone Roxane had never heard him use before. 'Of course I'm back. I told you I wouldn't be long.'

Toby's big blue eyes widened in sudden anxiety. 'Mummy?' he whispered querulously.

'Mummy will be back too,' said Gareth confidently, taking the small hands in his. 'But tonight you're going to stay with me, and we'll have cookies and fruit punch and I'll read you a bedtime story. OK?'

Toby eyed him speculatively. 'Play bears with me?' he asked.

Gareth stood up and swung the little boy on to his shoulder. 'That's blackmail,' he laughed. 'But yes, all right, I'll play bears with you if you'll be a good boy and go right to sleep when I say.'

'OK.' Toby wriggled happily and grabbed a handful of Gareth's dark hair.

'Ouch,' said Gareth, disentangling himself, and putting Toby down. 'Are you trying to make me bald?'

Toby found this idea so enchanting that he dissolved into hysterical giggles. A tall, fair-haired teenager who had been watching the scene from a chair in the corner rose to her feet and said she must be going.

'Thanks, Ann-Marie,' said Gareth, pulling some bills from his wallet. 'I appreciate yur help.'

'No problem,' replied Ann-Marie, eyeing Roxane curiously as Gareth opened the door.

Toby stopped giggling when the girl left and looked doubtfully at Roxane, who was standing indecisively by the window. 'Who dat?' he asked, pointing disapprovingly.

Gareth ruffled the blond curls. 'That's Roxane. She's going to play with us too.'

But when Gareth got down on all fours and started growling as he crashed around the apartment after a chuckling and shrieking Toby who kept shouting, 'Big bear can't catch *me*,' Roxane said she was going to be the mummy bear and see to the cookies and punch.

Gareth's kitchen was quite small, but everything was well-ordered and neat. There was not a great deal of food in the fridge, but Roxane had no trouble finding the fruit punch, which she poured into three large glasses, and the cookies—chocolate—which she arranged carefully on a plate.

When she returned to the living-room, the bear hunt was over and the two players were seated side by side on a sofa. Gareth had his arm around Toby and was reading aloud from a colourful Dr Seuss book—all about green eggs and ham. Toby was watching him with shining eyes, and beaming happily as he tucked himself closer to his big friend.

Roxane put down the plate and glasses and smiled. 'That's a good story, isn't it?' she said to Toby.

He nodded. 'Mm. Specially when Gaff reads it.'

She turned to Gareth, smiling and shaking her head. 'You're full of surprises,' she said. 'There's no end to your talents, is there?'

'Gaff can do *everything,*' said Toby admiringly, flinging his arms around his hero's neck.

Gareth pulled a face at Roxane over Toby's shoulder. 'You see,' he said. 'That's what I've been telling you all along.'

'Hm,' replied Roxane sceptically. 'Keep that up, and your head will get so big, it'll burst.'

Toby pulled back from Gareth's neck and studied him anxiously. 'No, it won't,' he announced, after a lengthy inspection. 'Gaff's head is just exactly right.'

Roxane completely agreed with him, but she wasn't going to say so in front of Gareth. Instead, she passed round the cookies, and when Toby had consumed most of them and been dissuaded from drinking a second glass of punch, Gareth bore him off to the bathroom to remove the chocolate-covered evidence from his face and hands.

A few minutes later Toby was securely tucked up in the bedroom, and Gareth was sitting opposite Roxane on one of the leather sofas.

'Hungry?' he asked, smiling at her in a way that made her heart lurch so hard, she was sure he could see it move.

'Not really. We had the cookies.'

'Well,' said Gareth easily, 'I'm not a gourmet cook, but I can manage spaghetti—or more bacon and eggs.'

Roxane jumped to her feet, feeling that if she sat here looking at Gareth much longer she would be unable to resist putting her arms around the tanned neck that showed so enticingly above his heavy brown sweater—or running her fingers through the thick, waving hair.

'You made breakfast,' she said hastily. 'Now it's my turn. Just tell me where everything is.'

In the end they made spaghetti and meat sauce together in the small kitchen, which didn't solve Roxane's problem at all, because now Gareth was closer than ever as they stirred the pasta, laid the table and collided head-on over the sauce. But Gareth only laughed, kissed her lightly on the nose, and made no move to take things further.

When they had finished eating, at the table for two which just fitted into the kitchen, they took their coffee into the main room and sat down—again opposite each other—on separate sofas.

Gareth said nothing, and Roxane felt suddenly uncomfortable. 'When did you fly in?' she asked, for the sake of something to say.

'Yesterday.' He grinned at her. 'Your gibe about crocuses and blizzards made me decide to manufacture urgent business out here.'

She didn't believe him. He wasn't the type to invent business that didn't exist for the sake of people and yellow flowers. 'It wasn't a gibe,' she replied untruthfully. And then, because the answer was suddenly important, 'How long did you say you were staying?'

'About two weeks, I imagine. Time for business *and* pleasure. Will you come skiing with me tomorrow?' He smiled disarmingly, and Roxane wished desperately that she could say 'yes'.

'I can't,' she replied, shaking her head regretfully. 'I have to work, remember.'

'Take the day off.'

Roxane gaped at him. 'Just like that? What would you have said if I'd done that while I worked for you?'

'I'd have fired you.' He was smiling as he spoke. But all the same, she knew he meant it.

'Then don't you think Mr Ryerson might do the same?'

He shrugged. 'Maybe. But that's not my problem.'

Roxane sighed helplessly. The man was impossible. He wasn't the brute she had thought he was, but he was still the most arrogant, self-centred man she had ever known. 'No,' she said patiently, 'it's not your problem, it's mine. Which is why I can't go skiing. I need my job—*Mr* Mardon.'

'Ah, yes, but I've already offered you another.'

'Haven't you filled it yet?' Roxane's amber eyes widened in surprise.

'Not yet.' He put his arms behind his head, stretched his long legs and stared at her expressionlessly. 'Annette's still doing it.'

Why was it that that funny, guarded look came over his face whenever he spoke of Annette? Come to think of it, she supposed she knew the answer to that. She frowned.

'Don't scowl, it doesn't suit you.'

Roxane made an effort and managed to force a smile.

'You're very good with children,' she said, changing the subject quickly.

'I ought to be. I was the eldest of seven brothers. And one sister who died.' His deep eyes went suddenly bleak and distant, and his voice cut like stone. The white scar which she had forgotten about earlier was all at once very obvious.

'I'm sorry. Was she very old?'

'She was four. A little golden-haired angel, with a smile that would break your heart.'

He really did love children. What a strange, enigmatic man he was.

'I'm sorry,' she said again. 'It must—is it—does it hurt you very much—to talk about it, I mean?'

He shook his head. 'Hurt? No, I don't think so. It still makes me angry though.'

Roxane could see that. 'Angry?' she asked. 'Why angry?'

He brought his arms down from behind his head and she saw his knuckles clench white against his thighs. 'Because if my mother hadn't had to work so hard, if my father hadn't walked out on us, Maggie would still be alive. That's why.'

Roxane shook her head worlessly, and Gareth went on in a harsh, grating voice, 'Mother cleaned offices at nights to keep the family going. I was working nights too, in a Toronto warehouse. I was sixteen at the time. Neil and Terry, my twin brothers, were only twelve. They were supposed to take care of the young ones. But they were pretty young themselves, and one night they got tired of babysitting and went to hang out with the gang on the corner.' Gareth's mouth twisted bitterly. 'The little ones were asleep with they left. But I guess one of them got hungry and tired to light the stove. The next thing Neil and Terry knew, the house—if you could call it that—was up in flames and the fire engines were screaming down the street. Neighbours managed to rescue the boys—but Maggie slept at the back—with Mother when she was home—and they couldn't get her out.'

'Oh, God,' cried Roxane, covering her face with her hands. 'Poor little kid. No wonder you're still angry.' Hastily she brushed away a tear. 'Your poor mother. And Neil and Terry. They must have felt so guilty.'

'Don't worry about those two.' His voice was harder than ever. 'They may have felt guilty at the time. Nowadays the state takes care of them more often than not.'

She lifted her head. 'The state? I don't . . .'

'You know. By order of the court I sentence you to—what was it last time? Six months for breaking and entering, I think. You see, my brothers came to the same conclusion I did. That you have to take what you want from life, and that they didn't want any part of being poor again. Only my methods happen to be legal—more or less—and a great deal more successful.'

'Yes,' said Roxane slowly, beginning to understand all too well the resentment and angry determination which drove this tough, aggressive, but sometimes surprisingly gentle man. She remembered him laughing as he hoisted Toby on his shoulder. No wonder he had little patience with people who whined and expected things handed to them on a plate. No wonder he hadn't understood that firing Dart's employees without notice was unfair and unkind. He probably thought he was dealing them a much better hand than life had ever dealt him.

Her big eyes full of sympathy, Roxane got up, walked

across the room and sat down beside him. 'I'm so sorry,' she said, putting her hand over his still clenched fist. 'I didn't mean to open old wounds.' She stared unhappily at the floor. 'Compared to your childhood, mine was incredibly easy. We weren't rich, but we were close, and my brother and I always had enough to eat, and nice clothes. I guess I just didn't understand.'

'You understand a lot more than you think,' said Gareth, turning to her with a smile from which much of the bitterness had gone.

'I don't know . . .' Roxane looked doubtful. 'But—well, at least you must be glad you can provide for your mother now. Make things easier for her at last.'

'I wish I could. But she died three years after Maggie did. Never recovered from the shock. After that, I brought up the kids as best I could on my own. Which in Terry and Neil's case wasn't very well.' He sounded more resigned than bitter now, and without thinking, Roxane put her hand up to his face to try to smooth the lines across his brow. In a moment his big hand had covered hers and he had turned her palm upwards and was covering it with kisses.

Roxane stared at his bent head, then lifted her other hand to touch the dark hairs curling at his neck.

Gareth stopped kissing her palm and rested it on her knee. 'Roxane,' he said softly. 'Roxane. Your name means "dawn", doesn't it?' When her eyes opened wide in surprise he explained with a wry, self-conscious smile that he had looked it up in a book. 'You *are* like the dawn to me,' he went on, his magnetic eyes holding her captive. 'A beginning. Something new and bright. I've never met anyone like you before. So lovely, and yet so—kind.'

'Oh,' whispered Roxane, not knowing what to say. Her

first thought had been to put her arms around his shoulders to give comfort, because if he had never met anyone with ordinary human kindness before, he must have been terribly deprived. Her second thought, unwanted and unbidden, was that if what he had just said was the prologue to a line of seduction, it was a remarkably original one. No man had ever troubled to look up her name in a book before.

But she was spared the need to respond just then because the telephone rang.

It was Toby's mother. *Her* mother was going to be all right and she would be over to pick up Toby in twenty minutes.

In fact she arrived in something under twenty minutes. Gareth placed the still sleeping, angelic-faced Toby very gently in his grateful mother's arms, and told her to call him any time she needed help, as he would be around for the next two weeks.

And a few minutes later Gareth and Roxane were alone.

They stared at each other, and when he held out his arms, she walked into them as though it was the only place in the world where she belonged. And that was the way it felt, as he pulled her tenderly against his body and ran hard fingers slowly, seductively, down her spine. Her hips were pressed to his thighs as his hands moved lower, and she could feel his need and desire for her in every delicious movement. And she knew that her need for him was just as great, and that whatever had happened, or not happened, in the past had all been leading up to this—to Gareth, whom she loved with all her heart. She still didn't know if he loved her, but at the moment it didn't seem to matter.

Gently he drew her across to one of the long leather

sofas and pulled her down on his knee. Amber eyes locked with ebony.

'I want you, Roxane.' He spoke very clearly, and the words sounded loud in the large, quiet room.

'Yes,' she replied simply.

With a groan, Gareth laid her back against the cushions and swung her legs on to the sofa. His mouth covered hers in a kiss that seared her with its passionate hunger as she pushed her hands beneath his thick sweater to caress the smooth skin of his powerful back. One of his hands was on her breast, circling, circling—and arousing. He lifted his head for a moment, smoothing the hair from her forehead as he stared smokily into her eyes.

'Gareth,' she whispered. 'I love you.'

Suddenly his body went very still, and gradually the glazed, smoky look faded. He looked at her almost as if he didn't know who she was, then with abrupt, jerking movements he pulled down her blouse, straightened her skirt, and sat up.

She stared up at him, puzzled and confused, her body still trembling with passion.

'What is it?' she asked, stretching out her arm, almost in supplication.

He ran his fingers through his hair so that it stood on end in a dark, waving crest which made him more desirable than ever—more vulnerable somehow, and younger. 'I can't,' he said harshly. 'Not to you.'

'What do you mean? I—want you to, Gareth.'

'I know. That's why it's not going to happen.'

She frowned, and fought back the tears that she knew were threatening to spill over. 'Is it because I said I loved you?'

'Maybe. Partly.' His voice was clipped, and he wouldn't

look at her.

'Gareth—you don't have to love me back. I didn't mean . . .'

'Christ.' He laughed bitterly, and she could see the sweat glistening on his brow. 'You were right, Roxane. I am a brute and a heel.'

'No. No, you're not. I was wrong, quite wrong.' Two big tears which refused to be held back rolled damply down her cheeks. Brushing them quickly away, she sat up and looked blindly round for her bag.

Silently, Gareth handed her a handkerchief. 'History repeats itself,' he said without inflection. 'Isn't this where I came in?'

Roxane nodded, blowing vigorously. 'Yes. It is. Are you going to say goodbye again, Gareth?'

She heard him swear quietly under his breath before he replied forcefully, 'No, I am *not*. Right now I'm going to take you home, say goodnight—and since you won't come skiing with me tomorrow—I'll pick you up after work.'

'Oh.' A great weight was lifted from her shoulders. At least he wasn't giving up on her entirely. Perhaps she would be better off if he did. But she knew she couldn't bear even the thought of that—so she smiled weakly and went to fetch her coat.

Half an hour later they were standing outside the door of her apartment. Gareth kissed her casually on the forehead, gave her hand a quick squeeze, and vanished with his usual speed down the stairs.

Roxane stood alone in her bare, unfurnished room and touched her fingers to the place where his lips had been. Then wearily she dragged herself over to the doors leading to the balcony, opened them, and let the cold air stroke her skin. It was only when she began to feel as if shards of ice were pricking at her cheekbones that she realised that tears of angry bewilderment were pouring unhindered down her face.

# CHAPTER EIGHT

IN THE morning, after a surprisingly untroubled sleep, Roxane was still bewildered, but no longer so desolate and unhappy that she was unable to face the problems which had seemed utterly overwhelming last night.

Loving Gareth was never going to be easy. She had known that from the beginning when she was still trying to convince herself that she hated him. Even once she had accepted that she loved him, she hadn't liked him much. Not until yesterday really, when she had seen him with little Toby. She smiled, remembering Toby's beaming, worshipful face, and the moment when she had realised her terrible ogre was only a gentle giant.

But as she absently made coffee and forgot to put butter on her toast, her mind moved on to the later part of the evening. Why had he suddenly rejected her? If he was only going to leave her again, perhaps it was just as well. But he *had* wanted her as much as she'd wanted him, she was as sure of that as she had ever been of anything in her life. Was it because she had said she loved him? He had said it was, partly, but that didn't make much sense, because if she loved him, and he only *wanted* her, surely that made everything easier—at least from his point of view. Or had he suddenly remembered she was a virgin? Not that she had ever told him that. But he had once called her a gullible virgin, so somehow he must have guessed.

No, that didn't make sense either, even if he was wary

of virgins, because if Nina had not interrupted them with her crimson horror that day in her old apartment, Roxane was sure he would have made love to her right there. The only question had been whether she would have let him—and she had an uncomfortable suspicion that she would. Even then, when she hated everything she thought he stood for.

She stared blankly at a piece of toast, wondering why it tasted different. Then, seeing its dry, unbuttered state, she started to laugh. Was this why people were reputed to waste away from love? Because they forgot to put butter on their toast, and poured their milk into the sugar bowl? She glanced at her watch. It was getting late.

The riddle of Gareth's inexplicable behaviour would have to wait until later—when he came to collect her after work.

Promptly at five Roxane closed the door of the office and stepped into the bright March sunlight. Mr Ryerson had already disappeared into the nether regions somewhere behind the cat-pens, and she knew he was now deep in a consignment of books on Zulu Wars and Weaponry.

She was stowing the office key carefully in her bag when she realised she was not alone in the car park. A tall figure with his hands deep in the pockets of expensive-looking, tan-coloured trousers was leaning against a familiar white sedan. Immediately across from him, an equally tall, but thinner figure, with two cats under his arm, was emerging from a small green car.

Roxane stopped dead. 'Hello, Gareth,' she said, looking from one to the other. 'I thought you were going to pick me up at home.'

'Then you were under a misapprehension.' He grinned at her and gestured towards the car. 'Hop in.'

'I can't hop in. I've got my own transport today. Also,' she added, looking dubiously at the other occupant of th ecar park, 'I seem to have Pumpkin and Eggplant.'

'Pumpkin and *what?*' Gareth's eyes moved incredulously to James's furry burdens.

'Eggplant,' said Roxane firmly. 'I'd forgotten they were coming. You're late, James.'

'Traffic,' replied James briefly, casting a sour look in Gareth's direction. 'And if your social life isn't *too* urgent, perhaps you could book them in now.'

'She's closed for the day,' snapped Gareth, before Roxane had time to reply. 'Come on, sweetheart.'

Roxane gave an exasperated sigh. Here was James, who was always the soul of politeness, making sarcastic comments about her personal affairs—and Gareth, who was rarely polite, being more authoritative and obnoxious than usual, just to score off James. Was she really the cause of all this masculine snarling and snapping? If so, it was a novel experience for her, and one she did not much appreciate.

'Stop it, you two,' she said irritably. 'There's no need to behave like a couple of overgrown apes. Here, James, give me the cats. Gareth, I'll meet you at home after I've settled these two for the night.'

Gareth shrugged, and she could see that his temper was barely under control. James surrendered the cats.

When Pumpkin and Eggplant had been safely installed in their pens, and Roxane had locked the door for the second time, she found Gareth still lounging against his car, tapping long fingers impatiently against his thigh. Roxane's stomach gave a delicious lurch. He did look terribly attractive, all scowling and virile like that.

It was only after James had slammed the door of his car

and driven off down the driveway that Gareth got deliberately into his sedan and agreed to follow her home.

That evening he took her to a very luxurious restaurant with a magnificent view of the harbour. He said he owed her some recompense for last night's spaghetti and meat sauce. Roxane replied that this was lovely, but so was spaghetti because, having an Italian grandmother, she had grown up on it. Gareth seemed interested, and after that she told him all about her family and childhood and what had brought her to Vancouver—until she saw his eyes fixed on her with a very strange expression, and remembered that his childhood had been anything but happy. Her breezy monologue came to an abrupt halt.

Seeing her bright animation fade so suddenly, Gareth felt a pang of regret. He knew what had caused her to stop talking.

'It's all right,' he said quietly, putting his hand over hers. 'I had some good times too, you know.'

He told her about the good times, playing with his brothers in the snow, building a fort among the backyard garbage cans with wood pilfered from a nearby lumberyard—getting away with it had been half the fun—and the Christmas before their father had walked out, when he had come home with a big Christmas tree and expensive presents for them all.

He even told her of his early struggles to rise above his beginnings, how he had worked his way, by sheer energy and persistence, to a management position at the warehouse—and how that had inevitably led to more money, successful investments, considerable wheeling and dealing and, eventually, to the takeover of Dart Express. Gareth said that had been the best time of all, when he was sure that the shackles of poverty had been shaken off for good, and he was the master of his own fate.

Roxane smiled, feeling that at last she was beginning to understand the demons which drove this vigorous, dynamic man—and she wondered if he would ever tell her about the bad times. How he had got that scar, for instance.

When he took her home that night, he again kissed her lightly on the forehead and made no attempt to come in.

The same thing happened every night that week. He took her to a hockey game, the movies twice, and on Saturday to a friendly Italian restaurant—in honour of her grandmother. But although they laughed and talked and enjoyed each other's company, there was a wall between them now which Gareth seemed determined not to breach. For her part, Roxane tried to be content with what she had, making the most of these days with Gareth because she knew they would soon be over.

On Sunday they drove up the Squamish Highway to Whistler Mountain. It was late in the season for skiing but, surprisingly, there had been a fresh snowfall the night before, and the mountains shone bright and crisp and pristine in the clean morning air. They held hands on the chairlifts to the top of Jimmy's Joker, and as they flew down the slopes of the steep run together, skimming the moguls and catching their breaths in exhilaration, Roxane thought that she had never been so gloriously happy in her life.

Afterwards they rode up to the peak, to sample the lofty slopes of the wide West Bowl, and she revelled in the sensation of freedom and speed and the sheer joy of experiencing it with Gareth.

By noon it was almost warm enough to sunbathe, and they collapsed together laughing in a snowbank.

'You look like a dissolute princess,' said Gareth, turning on his side to gaze admiringly at her red-suited body stretched out against the snow. 'Did you know there's a tiara of snow on your toque?'

'No,' laughed Roxane, brushing it quickly away, and thinking that to her he looked like the Prince of Devils in his all-black ski suit, with the goggles pushed up into his dark hair. 'I'm not in the least bit dissolute. And really I don't think I want to be a princess. I'm quite content to be me.'

'Yes, I suppose you are. That's half your charm.' He was serious now, and he touched a hand to her face. Their eyes held. Then suddenly he was lying half on top of her, pressing her back into the snow as his lips sought hers. And they were kissing each other with all the pent-up passion which they had held in check for so long.

'It's a good thing we've got all these layers on,' said Gareth a long time later. 'If we hadn't, I'd probably be up for indecent behaviour in a public place.'

Roxane wasn't sure it was a good thing at all, indecent behaviour or not.

That night Gareth made bacon and eggs again. She said it was her turn to cook for him, but he said he was damned if he was going to eat in a home with two hard chairs, one table . . .

'And a waterbed,' said Roxane involuntarily, and then turned a very bright pink.

'And a waterbed,' agreed Gareth impassively.

After the incident in the snow, Roxane had been sure he would make love to her tonight. But he didn't. The only thing that changed was that he suddenly became less reticent about his family. She learned that he cared deeply for the two brothers in gaol and was still determined to get them back on track.

'You could give them enough money so that they wouldn't need to steal,' suggested Roxane doubtfully.

'No, I could *not*.' His voice turned instantly hard. 'I made it on my own. They can damn well do it, too.'

Roxane didn't think it was the time to tell him that not everyone had his drive and determination. Especially as he was now announcing proudly that two of his younger brothers were at college, and the other two had good jobs. The youngest of all was married, and Gareth expected to be an uncle very shortly. Roxane heard the pleasure behind the casually spoken words, and thought that there was one baby who probably wouldn't have to make it all on his own. His proud uncle would see to that.

Later in the week, after an evening when they had been to a rather gloomy play about equally gloomy people, Gareth told her what it had been like growing up in his depressed, seamy neighbourhood, where every other family was on the dole, and rival gangs fought each other in the streets just for something to do. As she had suspected, he had got the scar in a street fight. One of many, in which he did not usually come out the loser. Looking at the powerful frame now, stretched out so casually in a chair, Roxane had no difficulty in believing that, when roused to physical retaliation, it would be an unwise man who made the mistake of getting in his way.

On the second Saturday, Gareth was due to return to Toronto. Early on Friday evening Roxane called up Nina.

'He's leaving,' she wailed. 'And I don't know if he'll ever come back. He seems to like me, but he hardly touches me any more, and we haven't even . . . I mean . . .'

'Yes, I know what you mean,' said Nina gruffly. 'Roxie, this isn't the nineteenth century. Why don't you ask him?'

'Ask him what?'

'Ask him why he's treating you like the original ice maiden—and casting himself as your friendiy local deep-freeze. Oh! Roxie, he's not . . .?'

'No,' said Roxane with deep conviction. 'He most definitely is not.'

'Right. Then you'd better try to seduce him.'

'I think I have. And it didn't work. Nina, if he was anyone else, I *would* ask him what's the matter. But he's so—so controlled sometimes, so cold and hard to approach. Other times he's . . .'

'Yeah, I know, other times the snake is a warm, loving glacier.' Nina had never revised her opinion of Gareth, and Roxane had given up trying to change her mind.

When Gareth arrived to pick her up that night, the first thing he asked her was where she would like to go since it was to be their last evening together.

So tonight, of all nights, the choice was to be hers.

Their last evening. Roxane swallowed the lump in her throat. 'Your place,' she replied without hesitation.

Gareth eyed her low-cut black dress doubtfully. It outlined every curve of her body, and the close-fitting skirt showed a tantalising glimpse of scarlet nylon through the discreet split up the side. It had cost Roxane the fortune she didn't have, and, seeing the dazed look in his eyes, she began to think it was worth it.

'All right,' he agreed, shaking his head as if to clear away a mist—or a dream. 'All right. My place it is. If that's what you really want.'

'It is,' said Roxane with conviction. This was her last night with Gareth. Whatever happened or, as was much more likely, did *not* happen, she was not going to share it with a restaurant or a theatre full of people.

'That's quite a dress,' said Gareth, as he helped her off with her coat.

'Do you like it?' She smiled coquettishly.

'Don't smirk like that. It makes you look like a floozie. And no, Roxane, I don't much like it, because it inspires primitive urges which I'm desperately trying to control.'

'Why control them?' There. It was out. And if that made her sound like a floozie as well as look like one, well, that was just too bad. She loved Gareth. And he was going away. She needed one night to remember—even if it had to last a lifetime.

He stood very still, his hands grasping her coat. Then he tossed it over the back of the nearest chair and took a step towards her.

'Do you realise what you're saying?' he asked harshly. Roxane could see his fists bunched tight against his thighs, and the dark eyes fixed on hers were hard. But, behind the steely control in his voice and his rigid stance, she sensed something else—a smouldering fire that was slowly burning its way to conflagration.

'Yes,' she said, returning his gaze resolutely. 'Yes, Gareth, I know exactly what I'm saying.'

He swore, not quietly this time, but very succinctly, and with a range and proficiency the like of which Roxane had never heard before. But then, she had not been raised by the language of the streets as he had.

Seeing her stare of open-mouthed amazement, he stopped abruptly. 'I apologise,' he said, not sounding as though he meant it. 'But if you're going to make suggestions like that, you have to accept the consequences.'

'Yes, but that charming demonstration of your verbal dexterity wasn't quite the consequence I expected,' Roxane informed him drily.

For a moment his jaw hardened. Then she saw his lips twitch slightly. 'I suppose it wasn't,' he said finally, in a voice which seemed to shake. 'Roxane, what am I going to do with you?'

'Well, I already told you . . .'

'Didn't you, though. God, sweetheart, that dress, that sexy, outrageous dress—and you, so sweet and innocent, offering me . . . Roxane, have you any idea what you're doing to me?'

'I hope so,' said Roxane demurely, folding her hands in front of her and giving him a look of provocative intimacy.

Gareth swore again, crossed the space between them in one stride and caught her around her hips. 'All right,' he said, burying his lips in her neck. 'All right, my lovely Roxane. God knows, I've tried, but if that's the way you want it . . .'

His hands roamed sensuously down the smooth silk covering her hips, searing her flesh through the thin material and making her gasp with pleasure. Her arms crept around his waist, freeing his shirt so that she could feel the smooth, taut skin of his back.

His lips sought her mouth and, still with his hands on her hips, he drew her towards the bedroom. Roxane had a brief impression of a very large bed covered in luxurious black, a mirror which took up almost all of one wall, and a collection of books, shoes and papers in a chaotic pile in a corner. After that she was only conscious of Gareth, as he stopped just inside the bedroom door and, with one arm around her waist, bent her body backwards and ran his fingers very slowly up the split in her black skirt. When he reached the top of the split he paused for a moment, gently massaging her leg through the thin nylon mesh. Roxane moaned and tangled her fingers in his hair as he moved beneath the skirt, pushing it up over her thighs.

Then they were lying on the thick, cream-coloured rug and the scent and feel of Gareth was all over her as his hand touched the inside of her thigh and his firm mouth covered hers, his lips and tongue probing and devouring as she returned his kiss with a fierce, hungry passion that until this moment she had had no idea was in her.

Now she was opening his shirt, running her hands frenziedly across his bare chest. And he was pulling the black dress up over her head.

'You're beautiful, my love,' he murmured huskily, as her bra, stockings and panties followed the dress in a careless heap of clothing somewhere behind her head.

'I love you, Gareth,' she whispered.

For a moment he gazed down at her, transfixed by the naked perfection of her body as his hands ran lightly and expertly over every part of her, tantalising and arousing. Then his lips found her breast, teasing and tasting. Roxane gave a small, pleading cry—and after that neither of them saw anything any more as, very gently, he took her and made her a part of him—as she knew he would always be a part of her.

They came together in a wild, wonderful explosion of delight that Roxane had not known existed. Just for an instant there was a sweet, sharp stab of pain, and then it vanished in a miraculous surge of light that made shooting stars and the eruption of volcanoes seem like the dying embers of a campfire.

And they never made it to the bed.

Hours later, after they had made love again and discussed the possibility of moving to the bed, and decided it wasn't worth it, Roxane and Gareth sat side by side on one of the leather sofas.

He was wearing red boxer shorts and his shirt hung open over his bare chest. She had not put the outrageous dress on again, and was wearing a brown silk bathrobe belonging to Gareth.

She looked at his strong, well-formed legs and thighs, and thought how beautiful he was. Every wonderful inch of him that she had just come to know so well. Then she raised her eyes to his profile, and saw there something shadowed and brooding. She lifted a hand to smooth away whatever gremlin was troubling him.

'Don't,' he said harshly, seizing the hand and pushing it away.

Roxane stared at him, aghast. 'What is it?' she asked. 'Have I done something wrong? Is it because I—let you love me?'

'Don't be ridiculous. Do you think I'm that much of an arrogant jerk?' He jumped restlessly to his feet and stalked out into the kitchen. 'Come on,' he shouted to her. 'We haven't even eaten yet. Let's put some food together.'

'I'm not hungry,' Roxane called after him.

'Tough. I am.'

Roxane sighed, and left him to work out his ill-humour by himself. She had no idea what was eating at him, but she could hear him slamming and crashing pots around in the kitchen, and she hoped that somehow that was therapy for his temper.

Apparently it wasn't. Half an hour later he produced a very passable omelette served with fried potatoes and a can of soggy peas. But they ate it more or less in silence, seated close together at the small kitchen table. Roxane's efforts to lighten his mood by making bright comments about the season and what the weather might be like when he got back to Toronto were met by a stony, glowering silence.

And she had wanted a evening to remember. It was going to be that, all right!

When they had washed and dried the dishes, still in ominous silence, Roxane decided to take the bull by the horns—or the snake by the tail, as Nina would probably say.

'Gareth,' she said quietly, putting a cup of coffee in front of him as he sat at the table with his head bowed over his hands, 'Gareth, this is crazy. You're leaving tomorrow, and I can't bear it if it ends like this. Why won't you talk to me? Tell me what I've done?'

He lifted his head and stared bleakly into her eyes. 'You?' he said scornfully. '*You,* my love? You haven't done anything at all.'

His love. He had called her his love again. She sat down carefully in the other chair and reached a tentative hand for his. 'If I haven't done anything,' she said slowly, 'why . . .?'

Gareth pulled away as though her touch was a burning poker. 'Oh, for God's sake! Don't you see, woman? You're not to blame for this disaster—in spite of that impossible dress.'

'Disaster? You call what happened a disaster?'

He ran his hand wearily across his brow. All the fight seemed suddenly to have gone out of him. 'No,' he said very quietly. 'It was the most wonderful experience of my life.'

'Then what . . . ?'

'But the problem, my very dear Roxane,' he continued as if she hadn't spoken, 'is that I'd no right to let it happen. It wasn't fair to you—or to—Annette. Not when I've made her a promise that she has every right to expect I'll honour. And not when I haven't had the—courage? decency?—to let you know the truth.'

'The truth?' Roxane was conscious that her face had

gone very white, and for some reason she was finding it hard to breathe.

'Yes.' Gareth's scar had gone whiter than her face. 'You see, Roxane, my darling, sweet Roxane, Annette and I are going to be married. Just one week from tomorrow, to be precise.'

Suddenly he lifted his fist and smashed it down on the table, and the scalding hot coffee tipped sideways and ran all over the floor.

# CHAPTER NINE

'GOD!' yelled Gareth, as the scalding liquid splashed down and spattered his knees and thighs. 'What the hell are you trying to do to me?'

Roxane took a long, deep breath. This was no time to tell the man who had just shattered her dreams that he was behaving like the arrogant jerk he had just assured her he wasn't.

She took a quick step to the sink, soaked a dish-towel in cold water and spread it, still dripping, over his reddening thighs.

'There, just keep your skin cold and damp, and you shouldn't burn too badly,' she told him, in a voice devoid of emotion.

Her finger brushed his hip, and he looked up briefly and met her eyes. Then he turned away again to stare fixedly at a small bird perched on a wire outside the kithen window. Roxane was still crouched at his feet on the floor, staring at the redness on his knees. She wondered if she should get another cloth, but her body appeared to have lost its ability to move.

After what seemed a very long time, the bird flew busily away. Gareth glanced down at Roxane's bent head and saw the soft brown hair cascading over her shoulders. He put out a hand to touch it. Then, with a visible start, he pulled it quickly away.

Roxane looked up. His face seemed bruised somehow,

filled with anger and pain. 'I'm sorry,' he said, in a curious blank voice. 'I shouldn't have blamed you because I spilled the coffee.'

'No,' said Roxane dully. 'You shouldn't.'

But it didn't matter. He had just broken her heart, and here he was apologising for shouting at her because he had burned his legs. A glimmer of anger began to worm its way into her battered consciousness.

There was another long silence, and then Roxane said bitterly, 'Don't you think you're apologising for the wrong thing, Gareth?'

'What?' He sounded puzzled, as though he really didn't understand.

She felt the anger flare again. 'You've just made love to me, Gareth. And as you say, you had no right to. It *wasn't* fair to Annette. You betrayed her trust—just as you betrayed mine.' On the last words her voice sank very low, and she felt as if she were shrivelling up inside—even as on the outside she was beginning to burn, with a steady, ever-increasing rage.

Gareth shifted restlessly in his chair. 'Roxane, get up off the floor,' he snapped, with devastating irrelevancy.

Biting her lip to keep from screaming at him, she did as he wished. She pulled herself to her feet and stood looking down at him—sprawled so casually in front of her at the table. Vaguely she noticed that he had removed the wet cloth and that his legs were beginning to return to their normal attractive brown.

'All right,' she said coldly. 'I'm off the floor. And I suppose now I'd better get dressed and out of your house.'

At that, he came startlingly alive. With breathtaking speed he sprang to his feet and caught her by the shoulder. 'No,' he said forcefully. 'Sit down. In a chair. I want to talk to you.' With scant consideration for her not very well-upholstered bottom, he shoved her on to the closest chair and turned the other one around so that its back was facing her. With his thighs straddled across the seat, he placed his forearms on the wooden back and fixed his deep eyes steadily on her face.

In spite of her growing hurt and fury, Roxane felt a familiar surge of desire. He might be a worse snake than even Nain had suspected—but in those shorts, and with his shirt hanging open like that, he was still the most gloriously attractive man she had ever met.

'OK,' he was saying now, in a hard, strained voice. 'First of all, my love, as usual you are absolutely right. Of course I wasn't fair. And I do apologise, from the bottom of my heart.' His fingers curled convulsively around a rung of the chair. 'But, my God, Roxane, I am a mere mortal —and when you practically threw yourself at me in that incredible black dress . . .' He shrugged, and his lips twisted wryly. 'I'm afraid it was more than flesh and blood could bear. And I am very much flesh and blood, you know.'

'I'd noticed,' said Roxane sarcastically.

He stared at her, his eyes black, shadowed pools. 'Yes. so you did. Roxane, if you'll listen to me for a moment, I'll do my best to explain.'

'Oh, sure,' she gibed. 'Dream up some fairy-story that you think I'm gullible enough to swallow. That's what you really mean, isn't it, Gareth?'

He raised his arm, and for a moment she thought he would strike her. Then he dropped it again and his normally expressive face became so still and cold that she felt her own flesh shiver and grow cool.

'No,' he said quietly, his voice as remote as spring on a storm-tossed, wintry sea. 'No, that's not what I mean at all.' He paused and ran his hand wearily over his eyes. 'I want to do what I should have done before. Tell you the whole, unvarnished truth. It's not an excuse, Roxane, because no excuse can possibly justify what I've done—but still, it is the truth.'

She felt a peculiar tightening in her chest, as if a hand was slowly squeezing all feeling from her heart. She was afraid of Gareth's truth—and she had lost the ability to trust him. But she nodded. 'All right,' she said very coldly. 'All right, Gareth. Say what you have to say.'

He swallowed, and she saw the sinews moving in his neck. His eyes were very deep. 'The first thing you have to know,' he began slowly, 'is that Annette and I have known each other for a very long time. We grew up in the same neighbourhood, and she's pulled herself up by the bootstraps in the same way I have done. Before I brought her out to Vancouver, she was the credit manager for a company in Toronto where she was very highly thought of. We'd been friends—more than friends—for years. When I moved, I asked her to come with me.'

Roxane nodded dully, not looking at him. 'I see. So you turned a perfectly efficient credit manager into an impossibly inefficient personnel one.'

Gareth shook his head impatiently. 'That's hardly the issue now, is it, Roxane? But yes, I gave her personnel because Foychuk had just retired and Dart already had a cracker-jack credit man. He's still with us. And until I met you I didn't think personnel involved more than seeing that medical premiums were paid properly, that raises were kept within reason and that staff arrived regularly and on time. But none of that matters now. Does it?' His eyes seemed to bore into her brain.

'No,' said Roxane. 'No, it doesn't. Was Annette your

fiancée then?'

He glanced at her sharply, the blank mask of his face cracking slightly. 'No. She wasn't. But we had an understanding.'

'I'll bet you did.'

'Stop it!' Gareth's voice cut across her misery like the slash of a knife. 'Stop it, Roxane. I want you to listen, and listen you bloody well will.'

'Why should I?' Roxane felt the pressure in her chest grow tighter as he reached across and grabbed her round the wrist.

'Because it matters, that's why.'

'Perhaps it matters to you . . .'

'It matters to both of us, Roxane.' His voice was so low and filled with such determination that in spite of herself Roxane was forced to listen.

'No, Annette was not my fiancée when we came out here. She was my admired and respected friend who had stood by me during some pretty bad patches in the past.'

'You said she was more than a friend.'

'Yes. That, too. And we intended to marry some day, when the time was right.' He glanced at his hand which was wrapped around her wrist, and abruptly let her go. 'I was in a very black mood at the time of the move to Toronto. Partly because I knew you were right about the way I handled Dart's move, and I didn't much like myself for it. And partly because everything else went wrong, too. The computer didn't take kindly to the move, and there were numerous problems at work. In my absence the decorators had painted my house solid pink, there'd been a break-in and half my furniture was stolen—and to top it all off my new housekeeper left in a huff over mice in the washing machine. And suddenly the time seemed right. I wanted some peace and order at home, I was ready to start a family. Annette was kind and . . .' he smiled sardonically 'consoling, through all my black bad temper. So I suggested we set the date. And she agreed. Then she said she'd like to quit her job.'

'So you tried to make me take it.' Roxane stared out of the window. The little bird was back, busily preening its feathers.

'Not at first. I interviewed several people. But none of them seemed right. And then I had a brainwave. For some reason I couldn't begin to understand—or didn't want to—you'd been in my mind at odd moments ever since I left Vancouver. I'd just shown out an applicant who couldn't make up his mind what socks to wear for the interview and had apparently decided on one of each, when your face came to mind again. And I thought I saw light at the end of the tunnel. A solution to my problem. When you turned me down I was angrier than I would have believed possible—and I couldn't understand why.'

He glanced at Roxane, but she was still staring, blank-faced, at the bird, so he went on steadily, 'The wedding plans were going ahead, but somehow the whole thing didn't seem such a great idea any more. I was restless and edgy, and Annette said perhaps I should clear up the business in Vancouver and get away from all the fuss and commotion for a while. She enjoys dealing with it herself, anyway. It was only when I was on the plane on the way out here that I realised I hadn't come to get away. I'd come to lay a ghost. You.'

'In more ways than one, I suppose. Thanks,' murmured Roxane acidly. Her chest was going to explode at any moment, and she knew that if she looked at him she was definitely going to scream.

'Don't mention it,' he said drily—and was quiet for so long that she almost turned around to see if he had gone. Then, when the silence became so oppressive that she knew she would *have* to move, he said softly, 'But the ghost wouldn't lie down, would it? I fell in love with you, instead.'

At that, Roxane did look at him. His strong, carved face was almost gaunt, and his eyes had a cavernous, empty look.

'And now,' she asked, equally softly. 'What now, Gareth? You're still getting married in a week.'

He shifted restlessly in the chair, gave her a bleak, hollow stare, and turned away again. 'I don't know, Roxane—but—yes, I suppose I must.'

The hand squeezing her heart let go so suddenly that every emotion she had ever felt for this man seemed to spill out with an almost audible cry. And then she realised it *was* audible as she heard her own voice, dripping with venom, say furiously, 'Yes, Gareth, my charming, irresistible, self-centred Gareth. Yes, I suppose you must. But don't lie to me. That wasn't the truth you just told me, was it? That was a lie—a lie to let me down gently, to ease your guilty—minimally guilty—conscience. Wasn't it? The truth is, you came out here on business, decided to amuse yourself with impulsive, silly little Roxane while your true love laboured on with wedding plans at home, and now that your little fling is over you're going back to her with a shrug and a grin and a promise to love her all your life—or until the next silly, impulsive idiot throws herself your way.'

When she first began to speak, Gareth's eyes had been clear and sombre, but as she went on, her voice rising sharply, they hardened and grew cold. She saw his lips draw into a straight, almost cruel line.

'It wasn't much of a fling, was it?' he jeered unpleasantly as she finished. 'One night out of two weeks. And you *did* throw yourself my way, didn't you, Roxane? Steamy seduction in black . . .'

Roxane could stand it no longer. 'You bastard!' she shouted, jumping to her feet and shoving the chair so hard that it fell over. 'You utterly unspeakable bastard. Don't you know that if I'd had any idea at all that you belonged to Annette, I wouldn't even have gone skiing with you—let alone to bed?'

'In case you've forotten, we didn't actually make it to the bed.' He was deliberately baiting her now. 'And just for your information, Roxane, I don't "belong" to Annette, to you, or to anyone else. I belong only to myself. That's the way it has been and the way, I assure you, it's always going to be.'

He had risen to his feet, too, and was standing over her. She was frighteningly conscious of his anger as he towered above her, tall and somehow threatening in the small, cramped room.

But in a moment her own fury wiped away all sense of the futility of trying to get the better of this large, aggressive man. How *dared* he jeer at her because they had made love on the carpet?

'Bastard!' she shouted again. 'I wish Annette joy of you. *And* luck. She'll need it—for the next time you find some moonstruck woman just waiting to be seduced.'

He stood very close to her, and when she looked up she could see the pores on his skin—and the white scar pulsing beneath the light. When he didn't speak, she drew herself up, lifted her chin and said quietly, from some reserve of dignity buried deep within her misery, 'Goodbye, Gareth. Next time you're back in town, don't call me, don't come near me. Don't even write. Because if you were the last man alive in the world, I still wouldn't want to see you. Not ever again.'

He stared down at her, and for a moment she was confused by the look in his eyes. A haunted, almost desperate look. Then his heavy lids partially covered them and all she could see was the blackness of his thick, arched brows.

Damn it, she owed this bastard one. The blood seemed to flow into her fingertips, and without thinking she drew back her arm to aim a blow at his face.

But he was too quick for her. The next moment her wrist was caught in an iron-hard grip, and before she realised what was happening he had drawn her towards him, his free arm was locked around her waist and he was kissing her—a long, hard, angry kiss that seemed to go on for ever. But it could only have lasted a few seconds. And in those few seconds all the familiar feelings came flooding back, and she thought for one brief moment that she was where she really belonged.

And then he was pushing her roughly away, his eyes no longer haunted, but dark, and filled with anger.

'Goodbye, Roxane—for the last time. By the way—if you're interested, you were right again. I *did* come out here to seduce you.'

Afterwards, Roxane never knew how she got out of the apartment, but Gareth had not been with her when she arrived home, so she must have taken a taxi. And she was wearing the black dress again, crumpled, ripped at one seam and very much the worse for wear. But it didn't matter at all, because she knew that whatever happened in the future, she would never want to wear it again. She pulled it off, remembering the fortune it had cost her and not caring.

Later it occurred to her that Gareth had done it to her once more. This time she had been the first to say goodbye, but somehow he had turned it around, and in the end he had been the one to make it final—and seal it with a kiss. She never had been able to convince him this was no way to say goodbye.

That night, as she lay in the big waterbed, for the first time aware of its size and loneliness, she thought about the evening that had just passed. In the beginning it had been the most wonderful evening of her life, the culmination of all her half-formed hopes and longings. And afterwards—it had crumbled into the dusty ashes of a dream which had barely begun.

To make things even worse, in the midst of her grief she was conscious of furious self-condemnation because she had, even for a moment, thought that she, and not Gareth, might be responsible for his behaviour. She had been fool enough to ask him what *she* had done. Bastard, she muttered to herself for the hundredth time that night.

As she stared into the darkness, and as rage and hurt died down and became nothing but empty desolation, it slowly came to her that Gareth might—just might—have been telling her the truth about his feelings. She remembered the dark desperation in his eyes and the speed with which his temper had flared when she told him she didn't believe him.

She had wanted to believe him, though—believe that he, who was used to knowing what he wanted and getting it, found it hard to accept that for once he had made a mistake. A major mistake. He had asked the wrong woman to marry him. And had he now realised too late that she was not what he wanted at all?

It was no surprise that he had reacted to that discovery by losing his temper. Her own reaction surprised her much more, because instead of accepting with dignity his decision to keep his promise to Annette, she had raged at him in a blind, unfocused fury. And, inevitably, that had made him hit back. His outbursts never lasted long though, she recollected. Not that it mattered. Not that anything mattered. Because she had told him never to come near her again. He rarely did anything he was told, of course. But this time he would.

Because this time he was marrying Annette.

It would suit him to remember Roxane as a pleasant, amusing interlude which had ended in angry words.

And was over.

Restlessly, feeling perspiration prick at the back of her neck, Roxane reached for the light. She needed the warmth of a lighted room. Somehow the darkness made everything seem worse.

She glanced idly at her watch. It was Saturday. One week from today, the only man she could ever love would be married to his blonde Annette.

She clicked the light off again sharply, because it hadn't helped.

Annette. She had always known Gareth was hooked up with Annette, but it had never occurred to her that their liaison was anything more than a physical convenience. And for some reason she didn't believe it even now. Indeed, during the last two wonderful weeks she had almost completely forgotten the buxom blonde's existence. So why was Gareth marrying her? And why had he told Roxane that he didn't belong to anyone—and that he had come out to Vancouver with only an easy seduction on his mind?

It was odd that he had waited two weeks to let it

happen . . .

She shrugged her shoulders against the pillow and turned irritably on her side. What difference did it make, anyway?

Gareth was going back to Toronto. And it was over, over, over.

The next day Roxane was late for work. After tossing her way into a restless sleep some time in the small hours of the morning, she had not even heard the alarm. Or perhaps she had, because when she finally awoke at nine o'clock, she found it lying half-way across the room with springs and screws scattered around it like shiny, accusing eyes.

Mr Ryerson was in a panic brought on by the telephone and an unfounded fear that Roxane had taken a sudden dislike to cats. She managed to calm him down with coffee, and he was so relieved to see her that no further reference was made to her unusual tardiness.

In the days that followed, she found she was quite unable to shake off a profound feeling of lethargy which seemed to sap her energy and prevent her from taking any interest in the world outside her immediate daily routine. Vaguely, at the back of her mind, she was aware that this feeling of blankness and uninterest was only a way of coping with a loss that was as real and final as if Gareth had actually died. And indeed he had, as far as she was concerned, because the Gareth she had come to love was only an illusion, a façade behind which Nina's snake in wolf's clothing dwelled.

When Nina came over to visit, her contentment and happiness with Jack was so obvious that Roxane felt a pang of quite unfamiliar jealousy. That brought her up short. Envy of another's happiness was an ugly emotion, one she had always despised. With characteristic frankness, she told Nina exactly how she felt.

Nina was only partly sympathetic. 'You've had a shattering experience,' she agreed, 'and being a little envious when you see someone else enjoying what you've lost seems perfectly normal to me. It's not a crime. But Roxie, you've got to do something to snap out of it. You're only twenty-three, and you *can't* let one rotten snake poison your whole life. You've got to fight back. Rise like a phoenix from the ashes.'

Roxane gave her friend a watery smile. 'Some phoenix,' she murmured. 'I feel more like a sparrow the cat dragged in.'

'Well, you look more like a sick owl some misguided dog brought in,' said Nina frankly. 'Roxie, why have you gone back to wearing those ridiculous glasses? And that white shade of powder does nothing for you at all. What's the matter with you?'

'Oh, Gareth's the matter with me, of course,' replied Roxane dully. 'And he said the same thing as you about my glasses.'

'Huh. For once the snake hit the nail on the head. But I'd just as soon he hadn't hit *you* on the head, which is what I think must have happened.'

'Of course he didn't. Gareth's not like that.'

'Not literally, you idiot. I mean you're acting as if you're got a crack in your skull. How can you expect to get over him if you skulk behind glasses and ghostly make-up?'

'How do you know I'm skulking?'

'Well, you are, aren't you? You figure if you make yourself as unattractive as possible, no man will come near you and you won't have to make the effort to get on with your life, get over Gareth—and maybe even be happy.' She eyed Roxane's bent head shrewdly. 'I'm right about that, aren't I?'

For a long time Roxane didn't answer. Then she lifted her head, looked her friend in the eye, and sighed. 'Yes. I think you are.'

'That's a start, anyway.' Nina smiled her relief. 'Come on now, we're going to get those contacts in, put some make-up on you—and you and I are going out to celebrate.'

'Celebrate what?' asked Roxane sullenly.

'Your resurrection. Come on, Phoenix.'

Over the course of the next few weeks, Roxane was indeed resurrected. And Nina began to regret that she had interfered.

From a morose recluse, Roxane turned into a giddy, frantic and, in Nina's anxious opinion, almost unbalanced butterfly.

It began one evening when she and Jack visited their neighbourhood pub and found Roxane there, sipping orange juice in the company of a red-haired man in a pink shirt and skin-tight black striped trousers.

'Hi, Nina,' cried Roxane in a high, strained voice. 'You remember Roger, don't you? He used to be a friend of Michael's.'

Yes, thought Nina doubtfully, and you always said he was a creep.

'We ran into each other in the supermarket,' explained Roxane, giggling. 'Literally.' She giggled again. 'He's taking me to a party tonight and I'm going to meet all his friends.'

Nina opened her mouth to point out that Roxane had met Roger's friends once before and had said they were worse than he was. Then she took note of her friend's long, swinging ear-rings, sexy scarlet jumpsuit and the pretty face unnecessarily smothered in make-up. Her eyelids too were smeared with so much purple shadow that the beautiful clear amber of her eyes was almost completely obscured. And Nina closed her mouth again, because this was a Roxane she couldn't begin to understand.

Roxane saw the disapproving expression on Nina's face and knew exactly what she was thinking. But she didn't care. Not any more. Nina had said she should rise like a phoenix. She glanced at the scarlet jumpsuit, recognised without interest that a slightly sleazy parakeet might be a more accurate description of her image—and found she still didn't care. It was better than skulking, anyway, through the empty years ahead. Her garish attire had attracted Roger, hadn't it? And Nina said she must learn to live without Gareth. If she couldn't have Gareth, Roger would do instead. Anybody would do, as long as she needn't think. Think or remember—dark eyes, not Roger's pale ones, firm, clean lips and a smile that warmed her heart . . .

She saw Nina and Jack turn away, glanced again at her companion, and gave him a bright, brittle smile.

Later that evening he took her to the party. The next night one of his friends took her out—in a passion-pink dress which she knew clashed with her complexion. But she danced frenziedly till the small hours of the morning, laughing and bubbling with a frantic energy that she was aware had every male eye in the room fixed on her in hopeful anticipation. But that was good, wasn't it? Other men might keep her mind off Gareth.

Vaguely, at the back of her mind, and as party followed party, was the knowledge that she couldn't keep this up. That the strain must eventually catch up with her. She was still making it to work, though often with deep bags beneath her eyes, and she was managing to get through the days with reasonable calm and stability. But the evenings were one made, shrieking social whirl.

They had to be. Because if she paused, or slowed down for a moment, immediately she saw Gareth's face in front of her eyes and the memories came flooding back. Along with the final memory. Of Gareth telling her he was going to marry Annette. And of her own response, when she had said she never wanted to see him again. Would it have made any difference if she had not told that incredible lie? No. How could it? By now he was a married man.

When the phone rang and a man she had met last night said he would be over in five minutes to take her out, she gave a theatrical laugh and said she couldn't wait.

'At least you're not drinking,' said Nina glumly, on one rare occasion when she agreed to accompany Roxane on her revels.

'Of course not. Why should I? I'm having a wonderful time without it.' Roxane's eyes were very bright and she was glancing around the room with a vague, disconnected air as if, for a moment, she was not even sure where she was.

'Roxie, you'll get yourself raped if you keep dressing like that, and hanging around with all these wild and weirdo people,' protested Nina despairingly.

'Raped?' said Roxane brightly, tilting her head coyly to one side. 'I think that might be rather fun, don't you?'

'No, I do not,' said Nina crossly. 'And what's more, neither do you. Roxie, where *do* you find them all?'

'Find my friends? Oh, all over. One friend leads to another. That sort of thing, you know.' Roxane giggled irritatingly, and with a resigned shrug Nina turned away. A moment later she heard Roxane laughing loudly on the dance-floor. When she looked around, a man in a black leather jacket and a beard was trying to put his hand down the front of her blouse. But, Nina noted thankfully, at least Roxane was pushing him away.

'What can I do about her, Jack?' she asked her lover later. 'I feel as though it's all my fault.'

'I don't know,' replied Jack fondly, putting a comforting arm around her shoulders. 'But if you've got any ideas at all, you'd better do something—fast.'

In the next few days Roxane received phone calls one after the other from Lisa, Martha, Molly and a number of her other old friends from Dart. All of them seemed to have survived the demise of their jobs, and either found new ones, didn't want new ones, or were confident of getting one soon. And all of them seemed curiously worried about Roxane and begged her to take life easy, come and see them—and be careful. It didn't take much to detect the well-meaning but clumsy hand of Nina behind all this sudden concern.

Roxane was mildly annoyed, but she recognised Nina's good intentions, told all the anxious callers she was fine, and proceeded to ignore their good advice.

Towards the end of May, when an early heatwave was making everyone's tempers short, and Mr Ryerson was muttering testily about air-conditioning—according to his wife he did this every year, so Roxane was not optimistic— she discovered one frantic Friday evening that she had made no plans for the following Saturday night. And in spite of the fact that she was desperately tired all the time now and could certainly use a night of rest and relaxation, she found the prospect alarmed her. A night to herself—to lie in a hot bath and soak—to feel warm and peaceful— and human.

No. She couldn't face that. Not yet. The time would come when she would have to confront her own humanity and learn to live as a total person again. And she would. Somehow she knew that, because she had been through bad periods before, and survived. None had been as bad as this, it was true, but sooner or later she *would* face life again and learn to carry on.

She stared round her still almost empty living-room. Yes, she would carry on—some day. But not now. Tomorrow was too soon. So tomorrow *she* would have a party. It was time she invited her new friends to her place for a change—and if the other tenants objected to the noise, they could come to the party too.

If worst came to worst, and the landlord kicked her out, she would cross that bridge when she came to it, she decided.

It didn't seem to matter any more.

And she forgot that she had once told Gareth to stop thundering on her door because the noise might disturb other people.

By the following afternoon everything was ready. Roxane had bought a supply of beer and wine, and told everyone who was invited to the party to bring their own poison if they wanted anything else. She had also acquired chips, nuts, pretzels and an impressive array of cheeses.

Surveying the table with its loaded plates of food, and the few pieces of furniture pushed back against the walls, she decided that everything was in order.

She wished she could do something about the weather, though. It was still extraordinarily hot for May, but the heat had now taken on a sultry, explosive quality which made her feel nervous and on edge—and there were dark clouds in the sky, ringed with an ominous yellow light. She shook her hair back restlessly. This was no time to give way to foolish fancies. In an hour or so people would start to arrive. It was time to peel off her jeans and slip into party attire.

Roxane inspected the contents of her wardrobe thoughtfully. She had worn the black velvet skirt with the slinky sequinned top last weekend, so that wouldn't do. And the green and white spotted dress was altogether too tame. Her eye fell on a crumpled heap in the corner. Seductive black silk with a tear at the seam. With a quick tightening of her lips, Roxane reached for a yellow and purple striped jumpsuit which she had been trying hard to ignore. It was loud, it fitted her like a tight, indecent glove, and she had known in the shop that it clashed horribly with her skin. But at the time she bought it she had been trying to prove something—to someone. She wasn't sure what any more, but she knew who the someone was all right. Gareth Mardon would hate that jumpsuit. She hesitated, and started to put it back, but the black dress in the corner caught her eye again, and with a sudden decisive movement she slammed the door of the wardrobe and, holding the jumpsuit high off the floor, carried it into the bedroom.

'Good grief,' gasped Nina, as she and Jack sailed through the door an hour later. She gaped at Roxane in glassy-eyed fascination.

'You look like a mutant wasp,' said Jack, with stunned but friendly honesty.

Nina shook her head. 'Silver-sprayed hair in a pompadour, purple and yellow satin—and Roxie, *pink* high heels. For heaven's sake, it's a good thing we arrived first. Let's get you into something decent before anyone else sees you.'

But Roxane was adamant. *She* thought she looked fine,

bright and cheerful and just right for a party—and she had no intention of getting undressed again.

Privately Nina thought she wouldn't have to. In a get-up like that, some man would do it for her. But no amount of coaxing from Nina or gruff cajolery from Jack could make Roxane change her mind. Nina noted the over-bright glitter in her friend's lovely eyes, and in the end she gave up in despair.

A short time later a group of laughing, chattering young people arrived. They were dressed casually but neatly, and didn't seem at all the type to cause trouble. Nina heaved a sigh of relief. Perhaps this party would be all right, after all.

The next group was louder, but still reasonably controlled. They were followed by a gang in a lot of leather and another group who looked in need of a bath. The room began to fill with smoke and the hot, steamy smell of too many bodies crammed close together. Roxane turned up the music and people gyrated and clutched each other in a frenzied pretence of dancing as the atmosphere in the room became as steamy and stifling as the weather outside.

Nina, who was hanging on to Jack as if he were her only bulwark against assault, looked anxiously around for Roxane. Then her eye caught a flash of yellow and purple in the corner by the kitchen, and she saw that her friend was backed up against the wall, her eyes very wide and flustered, as she tried to avoid the attentions of a blond, very good-looking young man in jeans and a cowboy shirt.

Grabbing Jack by the hand, Nina started to push her way towards the corner. But as she came up against a wall of bodies, there was a sudden loud rap on the door which could be heard even above the noise and music. The cowboy was momentarily distracted, and Roxane ducked under his arm. The bodies parted automatically to let her through and a gust of fresh air entered the room as some-one near the door swung it open.

It was the young couple from upstairs, complaining about the noise. True to her original intentions, Roxane beamed and asked them to come in. To Nina's faint sur-prise, they smiled happily and agreed, and two more gyrating figures were added to the crush.

A few minutes later there was another thump on the door and an irate man from two doors down the hall shouted that they had better keep the noise down or he was going to call the police. Roxane decided that asking him to join the party wasn't going to help much, and promised to do her best to keep things quiet. She turned down the music immediately, but it seemed to make very little difference to the noise level.

When the next indignant caller turned out to be the landlord, and they hadn't even heard him knock, Roxane came to the conclusion that she must have been tempor-arily unhinged to arrange this party, and that something really must be done at once.

She jumped on a chair, waved her arms and attempted to make herself heard above the din. Nina and Jack stood beside her and tried to lend support. But her calls for silence and attention fell on ears which deliberately tuned them out. Her frantic waving was met with jeers, more laughter and, in a number of cases, complete obliviousness to the fact that this was her apartment. Indeed, half the leering faces in front of her were those of total strangers.

Her eyes began to sparkle with frustrated, angry tears. If she couldn't get this lot calmed down quickly, someone really *would* call the police. Then she saw the cowboy who had been pestering her earlier standing by the sliding glass doors. She watched him take a bottle of beer in one hand

and smash its neck open against a wall. Sticky brown liquid ran on to the floor and splashed on the nearby glass.

Trembling with fury, Roxane stumbled off the chair, pushed past Jack and Nina as they tried to steady her and, squirming her way through the sweating throng, confronted the blond cowboy as he tossed back his head to drink from the broken bottle.

'Listen, you bum,' she hissed through gritted teeth, 'this is *my* apartment. I have to live here. And I don't need my walls decorated with your lousy drinks because you're too damn lazy to pick up a bottle opener.'

'Is that a fact?' the cowboy drawled rudely, putting one hand in the pocket of his jeans and leaning against the wall. His eyes travelled over her in a way that made her yearn to slap his leering face. 'So the timid kitten is a wildcat after all. How about that. Know what? You look sexy as hell when you're angry. You and me could make beautiful music together, honey.' He jerked his head at the bedroom. 'Anyone in there?'

Roxane drew in her breath, her eyes flashing amber fire. 'Get out,' she spat. 'Get out now. Before *I* call the police.'

The cowboy laughed. 'OK, spitfire. Whatever you say.'

Before Roxane realised what he was doing, he had grabbed her by the wrist with one hand, opened the sliding door with the other and dragged her through on to the balcony.

'Right,' he said nastily, shoving his face close to hers. 'I'm out. And just for good measure, sweetheart, so are you.' He slid the door closed behind him and she heard the latch snap into place.

Roxane glanced frantically over his shoulder into the lighted room. It was filled with people and movement, but there was no sign of Nina or Jack, and in the reflected glare from the windows it was unlikely that anyone inside even knew she was out here.

'Let me go,' she pleaded, as his arm looped over her shoulder. Surprisingly, he had managed to retain the bottle. Its coldness in contrast to the sultry night air made her gasp as it touched her low-cut back. 'Please,' she whispered, as his other arm circled her waist and she found herself pinned against the railing.

'Sure,' he said, 'I'll please you, sweetheart. Just wait till you give me a try.'

She could feel the bottle cutting into her skin now, and the railing was pressed into her back. Vaguely, she was conscious of a change in the noise drifting from the apartment. For a moment it seemed to swell, and she heard one loud voice roaring above all the rest. But the sound was muted by walls and windows and she couldn't hear what was being said. Then the furore appeared to die down again and it was quieter than it had been all night.

After that she lost interest in whatever was happening inside, because clammy fingers were stroking her throat, hot, boozy breath was in her nostrils, and wet lips were pressed sickeningly against her mouth.

'Don't,' she choked, wrenching her head away and struggling to get free. 'Please don't . . .'

'You mean don't stop, don't you, sweetheart?' His voice was hoarse, and thick with drunken lust.

'No, no, I don't want . . . *please*.'

'I *know* what you want, you little teaser.'

Roxane squirmed futilely and tried to break away. And then, as his hand slithered down the front of her jumpsuit, she was suddenly aware that the door behind him was no longer closed, and she opened her mouth to scream.

'I *know* what you want,' he repeated.

'And I know what *I* want,' a voice roared across the darkness, 'I want to break every bone in your filthy body, you unspeakable little swine.'

It was the most welcome voice Roxane had ever heard in her life.

Afterwards she couldn't recall how it happened, but one moment the cowboy was standing over her, breathing hot, smelly breath on her face. The next he was splayed against the opposite wall with Gareth's hand at his throat.

And he really isn't so little either, thought Roxane in dumb astonishment. It's just that Gareth is so large—and so angry. So very, *very* angry.

'Get out,' he snarled, releasing the cowboy reluctantly. 'Get out now, you lowlife—before I break your neck.'

This time Roxane's tormentor needed no second urging. With an eye fixed warily on Gareth's fists, he sidled past him into the apartment—which, she noted in startled disbelief, was now quiet and almost empty. Only Nina and Jack were still there, stoically attempting to tidy the debris.

Roxane pushed herself weakly away from the railing. There was something warm, sticky and wet trickling unpleasantly down her back. She looked up doubtfully into her rescuer's furious face, and the thunder which had been threatening all day erupted suddenly in a tremendous, rumbling crash as huge drops of rain began to splatter against the walls.

'Hello, Gareth,' she said cautiously, in a voice that was barely audible above the reverberating roar. 'Thank you for coming when you did.' When he made no answer, but only continued to glare at her, she added unhappily, 'When did you get here, Gareth? I'm afraid I didn't hear you knock.'

# CHAPTER TEN

GARETH'S eyes narrowed slightly, but he made no other sign that he had heard her. He was leaning against the wall now with his hands deep in the pockets of his jeans—almost as if he needed to restrain them.

Roxane shivered in the murky night air. How typical of him to reappear with the crack of thunder to herald his arrival. She studied the dark blue T-shirt stretched tightly across his chest, then forced herself to look up. He was regarding her as if she were an unpleasant piece of rubbish—or a particularly imbecilic child. Why? What had she done—or said, to make him look like that? Then she remembered her remark about not hearing him knock.

Of course. It must have sounded inane. He had just rescued her from the unwanted attentions of a drunken lecher, and here she was babbling like a bird-brained society hostess—if society hostesses ever wore unlikely satin jumpsuits and silver-sprayed their hair.

The release from tension was suddenly overwhelming, and as the irony of the situation swept over her Roxane started to smile. Ever since she had known him she had been trying to persuade Gareth to knock on doors quietly. And this time of all times, when she had needed him most of all, she had not even heard a tap.

Her smile widened. But there was no answering relaxation of Gareth's grimly set lips, and slowly her own smile faded.

'I did say thank you,' she murmured, as the silence became awkward and oppressive.

'Yes.' His voice was like the crack of a rifle. 'You did, didn't you?'

Roxane swallowed. 'Why are you looking at me like that? I didn't *let* him do it, you know. I was trying to get away.'

His mouth curled contemptuously. 'Oh, I believe you, Roxare. But the open invitation was there.' He gestured at her satin striped jumpsuit, and she could see the scorn in his eyes.

'I'm sorry you don't like my outfit,' she said tiredly. 'To tell you the truth, I don't like it much myself. But . . .' She hesitated. 'Gareth, I don't mean to sound ungrateful, but is it really any of your business what I wear?'

'It may be.'

'I don't see . . .'

'You don't have to see.' He turned his head abruptly, and for the first time Roxane realised that the cowboy's broken bottle must have slashed across his face. There was blood on the blue of his T-shirt and the white scar now extended down his cheek. Only the lower part wasn't white at all, it was an ugly crimson gash.

Roxane gasped, forgetting everything except that Gareth had been hurt. 'He stabbed you,' she cried out, stumbling frantically to reach him. 'Gareth, darling Gareth, are you all right?'

He stared at her as she reached a shaking hand up to his cheek, and a curious, uncertain expression flickered across his face.

'Yes, I'm all right,' he said gruffly. He moved quickly away from her anxiously probing fingers, but his voice was softer now, less harsh. 'Come on. We'd better help your friends with that unholy mess.'

Taking her arm, he pushed her ahead of him through the still open sliding doors.

Then behind her she heard him utter a word that made her ears burn. It was followed by a string of other words, whose meaning she was not anxious to discover.

Jack and Nina stopped what they were doing abruptly. Roxane half turned towards the cause of their astonishment. 'What is it?' she asked quickly. 'Gareth! Stop it.'

He stopped it as suddenly as he had begun. 'Your back,' he grated roughly. 'That bastard cut you too. You little idiot, don't you even realise you've been hurt?'

'Oh, have I? I thought I felt something trickling down my back. I expect it's only a scratch.'

Nina and Jack both came over to investigate. 'It won't look too bad once we've washed all the blood away,' announced Nina with calm practicality. 'Come on, Roxie. Let's get you properly cleaned up.'

'Gareth's hurt, too,' said Roxane hastily. 'We'd better see to him first.'

'Like hell,' snapped Gareth. 'Do you need any help with her, Nina?'

Nina shook her head. 'Not at the moment. Three of us in that bathroom would be just too cosy for words.'

'Make it four and we'll have an orgy,' suggested Jack, laughing at her as he returned to scraping cheese off the door.

A few minutes later Roxane and Nina emerged from the bathroom. Roxane's back had been sponged clean and a small piece of plaster covered the place where, happily, the bottle had only grazed her.

'Right,' said Nina. 'You next, Snake.'

For the first time since he had returned, Roxane saw the glimmer of a smile on Gareth's handsome face.

'Are we going to be cosy in the bathroom, too?' he asked, giving Nina a wicked leer.

'You are not,' laughed Jack from the kitchen. 'Try it and I'll rub turpentine in that wound.'

'No, you won't,' said Nina firmly. 'Come on, Snake. Into the bathroom with you.'

'I can hardly wait,' Gareth grinned as he followed her across the room.

'Hey, just hold it a minute, you two.' Jack advanced from the kitchen waving a threatening broom.

'And we're leaving the door *open*.' Nina gave both of them a no-nonsense glare and told Gareth to stand still so that she could inspect the damage effectively.

Roxane, momentarily alone in the centre of the littered living-room, heard Gareth murmur glumly that being ordered about by bossy women was the story of his life.

My eye, she thought. That would be the day when anyone, male or female, succeeded in bossing Gareth. But speaking of Gareth and bossy women, where in the world was Annette?

When he reappeared with Nina, with whom he seemed to be on amazingly good terms, the cut on his face no longer looked so bad, and it, too, was neatly plastered over.

But Roxane still had no idea why he was here, and she suddenly wished he wasn't. Because any minute now he would tell her he was going back to Toronto—to Annette—who was now his wife.

'What are you doing here?' she asked dully. She was tired and drained after all the drama, but she had to know the answer.

'Rescuing you from the Loathsome Cowboy, apparently.' His tone was still definitely grim.

'The Loathsome Cowboy?' She looked up at him, wanting to smile, but expecting to see only that look of scorn on his face. But, to her surprise, he was half smiling too.

'Mm.' He nodded. 'Your friend Nina there seemed to think you might need rescuing.'

Nina, who was kneeling on the floor sweeping up pretzel crumbs, cleared her throat uncomfortably. 'I'm sorry, Roxie. I know I have a terrible tendency to meddle. But I couldn't bear seeing you so unhappy. So I wrote to Gareth in Toronto.'

'But—Nina, I don't understand. You've never liked him. You said I was better off without him. And besides—he's married.'

'Don't mind me,' said Gareth. 'Talk about me all you like. Just consider me part of the furniture.'

'They always do,' murmured Jack sympathetically.

Nina ignored both of them. 'Well, it's true I didn't like him. But that wasn't the point. You did. And something you said made me think . . . Anyway, I wrote to him. And here he is. And I must say I've been forced to revise my opinion.' She grinned. 'You should have seen the way he cleared out that mob, Roxie. Jack and I kept trying to shut them up after you disappeared, but we weren't having any effect at all. Then Superman here came crashing through the door, couldn't see *you* at once but *could* see what was going on, let out a roar like an enraged bull elephant, grabbed the back of a few necks and the seat of a few very startled pants—and the next thing we knew, the room was cleared, and all that was left was the rubble. It was an impressive performance. It's a shame you missed it.' She grimaced. 'Your snake has teeth, Roxie.'

'Fangs,' muttered Roxane gloomily.

Behind her she heard a snort, and then she felt Gareth's hand on her shoulder. 'OK, Miss Razor-tongue. Let's cut the repartee and get on with cleaning up this mess. Nina and Jack have done wonders—but it *is* your responsibility.'

Roxane couldn't argue with that. 'Yes, it is,' she agreed, as she started to pick up plates and bottles. 'Of course it is. But it's not *your* responsibility, Gareth. You weren't even here to enjoy it.'

'For which small mercy I suppose I may be thankful. And don't talk nonsense. You and I have to have a long and serious chat. And I don't propose to have it surrounded by decaying food and the remains of your Bacchanalian revel.'

'Some revel,' grumbled Roxane.

'Quite. So this time, and this time only, I am helping you to clean it up. And if you ever try it again, I shall sit you down in the middle of it and dump the entire stinking mess on your head.'

Roxane didn't doubt he would. But as she scraped and scrubbed and swept, the one thing which stayed in her mind was that he was talking as if they had a future together. But they couldn't have. Unless . . . Had he come back to Vancouver to ask her to be his mistress? She supposed it would be just like him. A wife in Toronto, the children he wanted—and in Vancouver the woman he could keep as his plaything, his little bit of fluff on the side.

Clamping her lips together, she picked up a wet cloth and scrubbed so hard at a stain on the wall that all the paint came off too.

An hour later the apartment was almost restored to normal, although Roxane knew she would have to recompense the landlord handsomely for the paint. Jack had gone to start the car, and Nina, with a quick hug for Roxane and a friendly handshake for Gareth, said she knew they had a lot to discuss so she would leave them to get on with it.

'I'll be back in two days,' she warned them. 'And I don't want to find a war zone. Love, peace, and goodwill to each other are what I expect to see.'

Roxane closed the door quietly behind her. Then she turned around to face the man she loved.

'Well?' said Gareth, raising his heavy eyebrows. His hands were resting on his hips, and his eyes issued a challenge—and demanded an explanation.

'Well, what?' snapped Roxane. She was not going to let him browbeat her again. If he thought she had been behaving like an idiot, he was right. But what she did was no longer his concern.

He gestured irritably at the lurid jumpsuit, then waved a hand at her silver hair, which had long ago broken loose from constraint, and hung in an untidy tangle about her shoulders. 'That appalling garment you're wearing. And that rat's nest which used to be your hair. Why? And why the sleazy party—and your cowboy?' He ran a hand distractedly through his hair. 'I don't understand, Roxane. None of this nonsense is you.'

'No,' said Roxane, not looking at him. 'No, I don't suppose it is. Even Nina noticed my clothes were too bright.'

'Then for God's sake, woman, what in the devil got into you?'

When she didn't reply, he crossed the space between them in one stride and grabbed her by the shoulders. 'I want an answer, Roxane. And I want it *now*. Look at me.'

Roxane didn't want to answer. Nor did she want to look at him. Because the answer to his question was very simple, and giving it to him would accomplish nothing whatever—except perhaps to put another weapon in his hand.

'Roxane.' He was shaking her now, gently, but she knew he was determined to make her speak.

And what did it matter? He probably knew already, and putting it into words could make no difference.

'All right,' she said wearily, 'All right, Gareth. I'll tell you. Of course none of this is me. But you see, I didn't want to be me any longer, because "me" had loved—and lost—you. So I wanted to be someone else.'

Her eyes were riveted on the blue of his T-shirt, but now she felt his fingers move beneath her chin as he lifted her face so that she had to meet his eyes—which were so dark and deep that the expression of tenderness which softened them was almost hidden. Almost, but not quite. And conflicting with the tenderness were other emotions. Regret, guilt, desire and—love?

She closed her eyes. It wasn't possible. He couldn't love her, or he wouldn't have married Annette. But when she opened them again the look was still on his face, and he was smiling at her, a twisted, gentle smile that made her want to take him in her arms, put her fingers in his hair and pull that glorious mouth down to her own.

So she did.

Several minutes later, Gareth lifted his head, ran his hands searchingly over her satin-clad body and remarked that she was sticky with beer. 'And there's a pretzel in your hair,' he added, removing the intruding morsel with a tug that pulled down the rest of her pompadour.

He stepped back and looked her over carefully. 'You're a fright,' he announced, after careful consideration. 'A monster in yellow and purple. If I met you outside on a dark night, I'd run like hell.'

Roxane smiled weakly. 'I know I am. But I don't think I believe you'd run away.'

He regarded her judicially. 'No,' he said after a while. 'I wouldn't. I'd throw you in the nearest shower—which is exactly what I'm going to do now.'

He lunged towards her and she jumped away from him, laughing.

'Oh no, you're not,' she said, darting into the kitchen.

'Oh yes, I am.' He followed her and, as she pretended to reach for the frying pan, she felt his arms circle her waist from behind. Unthinkingly she laid her head back on his shoulder, and with her guard weakened, he spun her around to face him, unzipped the back of her jumpsuit at a stroke and began to push the straps down off her shoulders.

'Hey, what do you think you're doing?' Roxane was indignant. 'I've had quite enough of groping for one night.'

'I am *not* groping,' replied Gareth. 'Although the one idea the Loathsome Cowboy had right was to get this revolting object off your back.'

'Well, if that's not groping, I'd like to know what it is,' scoffed Roxane, as the offending garment fell about her feet, leaving her suddenly exposed and vulnerable in a lacy white camisole, panties—and pink high heels.

Gareth stared at her, and she could see the look of desire flare in his eyes again and the way they deepened as she hugged her arms across her breasts and tried to move around him.

'It's washing,' he replied, in answer to her question. 'Specifically, washing *you*.'

He put out an arm as she attempted to sidle past him. 'Oh no, you don't,' he said firmly, hauling her scantily clad body tightly against his chest.

Roxane successfully fought off an urge to give up all resistance and collapse blissfully into his arms. 'That is *not* washing,' she said sharply, as Gareth's fingers trailed softly over the bare skin of her back. 'It's groping—without an invitation.'

Gareth chuckled and removed his hand abruptly. Then he held it up to his nose and made a face. 'I thought so. Essence of beer and pretzel. Thanks all the same, sweetheart, but I don't think I want an invitation just yet.'

Roxane contemplated kicking him, thought better of it, and opened her mouth to tell him he was unlikely to get one anyway. Then she closed it quickly as he lunged at her again.

'Let me go!' she cried, as one strong arm swept behind her shoulders, the other locked around her waist and she found herself lifted against his body as if she were one of his lighter courier bags being swung aboard a plane.

'Not on your life,' he said, laughing. He strode through the living-room, into the bathroom, and dumped her unceremoniously upright in the bath. Somewhere en route, both her pink shoes fell off.

When he started to adjust the shower head and pull the curtain, Roxane decided it was time to make her bid for independence—because it looked suspiciously as if Gareth intended to scrub her down himself. And although a shower was exactly what she wanted, and the thought of sharing it with Gareth was almost too stimulating, the fact was that he was married—and being an 'other woman' had never been part of her agenda. Nor was it now, and nor would it be in the future—however much she wanted it to be.

Her spirits, which for the last half-hour had been lighter than they had been in weeks, dropped suddenly down to her toes.

'Gareth, I can manage very nicely on my own,' she said

firmly. Her voice held a note of quiet determination.

He was reaching for the soap, but he stopped when she spoke, studied her face searchingly, then nodded. 'All right,' he agreed.

Before she had time to think, she saw his face light up with a sudden devilish amusement, and as he closed the curtain, the last thing she glimpsed was his wicked grin as a shower of ice-cold water streamed down over her still partly dressed body—and she let out a howl of angry shock.

'Beast!' she screamed after him, as she leaped away from the chilling cascade and scrabbled frantically for the tap. But there was no answering jibe, and she wondered if he had heard her.

Right, she thought grimly, as the now blessedly warm water thawed her frozen body and she peeled off the sodden remnants of her clothes. Just you wait, Mr Gareth Smart-Aleck Mardon. Because you're not getting away with this without a scratch.

For the moment her depression of a few minutes earlier was drowned out by her dreams of revenge.

When she was ready to emerge from the shower, Roxane felt a stab of *déjà-vu,* because once again she was marooned in the bathroom with no clothes, and Gareth was lurking somewhere outside the door. But this time, by a stroke of good fortune, she had left her yellow-gold bathrobe hanging on a peg on the wall. Wrapping it round herself securely, she reached for the handle of the door.

Then she stopped. Surprise was the secret of a successful attack, and once she left the sanctuary of the bathroom, and Gareth had his eyes on her, her chances of mounting a triumphant revenge for her cold shower would be enormously diminished. She looked around thoughtfully and her eye fell on an empty bottle of spray cologne. Yes. With that discreetly hidden behind her back, it shouldn't be difficult to manage a sneak assault. Smiling smugly, she filled it to the top with water and stepped cautiously through the door.

She had not put her glasses on, but Gareth seemed to have vanished. Had he left, then? She was about to turn back into the bathroom when there was a sudden movement behind her, and she found her wrist manacled in an iron grip. The cologne bottle was firmly removed from her fingers.

'Nice try,' said Gareth approvingly. 'But you can just forget it, my love.'

Roxane turned to him with a look that reminded him of a pouting little girl who had been denied a promised treat. 'That's not fair,' she grumbled. 'I wanted to even the score.'

'It's perfectly fair. And *I* just evened the score. Remember that bath you gave me—the day I closed down Dart?'

'Mm.' A reminiscent look came into Roxane's amber eyes, and he saw her begin to smile. 'You did look furious, you know,' she told him. 'I thought you were going to murder me right there.'

He grinned. 'I did consider it. But somehow it would have lacked style, don't you think? Murder Outside the Ladies' Room just doesn't have the right ring to it, does it?'

Roxane laughed and gave up. 'All right, you win,' she conceded. 'Let's say we're even and call it a truce.'

'Yes. Let's.' The look he gave her made Roxane's stomach turn a somersault, and she pulled her eyes quickly away.

His arm came around her shoulders. 'You look so warm and vulnerable, all clean and sweet like that.' His voice was soft as velvet and his lips were close to her ear.

And suddenly she wanted quite desperately to cry. She turned to him a face so stricken that his dark eyes deepened with alarm.

'What is it, Roxane? Don't look at me like that. Don't you know I wouldn't hurt you for the world?'

She shook her head, for the moment bereft of speech, and he put both arms around her then and held her against his chest. In a minute, although she made no sound, he felt a dampness on his sleeve where her head was bowed dejectedly over his shoulder.

'Can we talk?' he asked gently.

Still she made no answer. His forehead furrowed with concern.

'You're too tired to talk, aren't you?' he murmured. 'You must have had quite a day. We'll leave all that till tomorrow then, shall we? Right now I'm going to put you to bed.'

At that, Roxane did speak. She looked up anxiously, and tried to push him away. 'No,' she said quickly. 'No, Gareth. We can't.'

'Who said anything about "we"?'

'But . . .'

'It's all right.' He was leading her determinedly across the floor. 'You've nothing to worry about. Just get some sleep now, and we'll talk it all out in the morning.'

'But . . .'

'Stop saying "but". Where's your nightgown? Or don't you wear one?' Behind the softly spoken words, Roxane heard an echo of his old derisive banter.

'Of course I do!' she said indignantly, roused from the

lethargy which threatened to overcome her.

'Pity. No, don't bite my head off.' He held up his hand, laughing as he saw the quick flash of anger in her eyes. 'I was only joking. Ah, I see, here it is.' He pulled a short blue cotton nightgown from beneath the pillow, and before she could stop him he had unfastened the yellow robe and slipped the cotton shift on over her head.

'There,' he said, as she sat blinking at him in amazement. 'Now let's get you settled for the night.'

In a moment he had pulled down the covers, swung her unresisting legs up off the floor, and tucked her neatly into the bed.

It did feel like the perfect place to be. The rain which had been pounding on the roof ever since Gareth's return seemed to have given up at last—and her eyes were terribly heavy. But she couldn't go to sleep. Not now, with Gareth in the room. He had said he wanted to talk. But there was nothing to talk about, was there? She closed her eyes in despair. Gareth . . . Talk . . .

Roxane blinked and came awake. That was odd. It wasn't dark any more, and she could hear rain pattering at the window. Funny, she thought the rain had stopped . . . Never mind. She felt warm and happy and secure, and for the first time since she had bought it, the waterbed did not seem too large and empty. She smiled. There was a nice, comforting arm wrapped around her body and her head was pillowed on smooth, lightly tanned skin . . .

Oh, my God! She gasped, pushed frantically at the arm, and sat up.

'Whatsa matter?' The owner of the body beside her stretched sinuous muscles, turned over on his back and slowly opened his eyes—which fell immediately on

Roxane, sitting up in bed with the covers pulled protectively up to her chin and an expression of stark horror on her face.

'Whatsa matter?' he repeated lazily, remembering with approval the slim, soft figure which the covers so successfully concealed.

Unwillingly, Roxane turned. She stared down at him, and what she saw made her swallow very hard. The thick, dark hair was ruffled over the pillow, the plaster on his face made him look like a wounded hero, and his glorious, sensual lips were smiling in just that way that was calculated to melt the blood in her veins. And to make this devastating vision irresistible, the sheet was pushed down to below his waist where, thankfully, it lay twisted about his hips. She saw the broad expanse of his chest, with not too much dark hair, but enough . . . She swallowed again, and passed her tongue over her lips. No. This was no good. It wouldn't do. It just wouldn't do at all. Gareth was a married man—and from the looks of things, he had just spent the night in her bed.

'What are you doing here?' she asked carefully, wrapping the covers more securely around her neck.

'What am I doing where?' He was still smiling that lazy, impossible smile.

'Don't play games with me, Gareth. What are you doing in my bed?'

He moved his head to one side, made a face, and pretended to consider the question. 'Well, I *was* sleeping,' he said slowly. 'But now—I can think of much more stimulating alternatives.'

'Stop it.' If Roxane had been standing, she would have stamped her feet. 'Answer me truthfully, Gareth. *Why* are you lying in my bed?'

'Truthfully? Because there was nowhere else to sleep, and I didn't want to leave you alone. After a riot like last night, you never know who might take it into his head to come back and try to cause trouble.'

'Oh, I see. And we didn't . . .?'

'Very flattering. Do you mean to tell me you would have forgotten?' He glared up at her reproachfully. Then, seeing the look on her face, he stopped teasing and added seriously, 'No, my love, we didn't.' When she continued to gaze at him with the face of an angel who has just discovered she isn't fallen after all, he propped himself up on one elbow and asked quietly. 'Would it matter so very much if we had?'

Roxane looked away. She couldn't bear those eyes on her any more. 'Yes,' she said distinctly. 'It *would* matter, Gareth. You're married.'

There was silence in the bedroom for a long time after that. Roxane was still gazing at the wall, and Gareth lay very still. When she felt his hand cup her face, she tried for a moment to resist. Then he had pulled her head round to face him, and she saw his eyes again—deep, intense and filled with a painful sincerity she had never seen in them before.

'I'm *not* married, Roxane.' His voice was very deep, every word enunciated clearly. 'I couldn't go through with it, you see.' He paused, and moved his elbow so that it brushed against her thigh beneath the covers. 'I thought I could, of course. But I knew the moment you told me you loved me, that night when we looked after Toby, that all my restlessness and confusion and just plain filthy temper meant one thing and one thing only.'

Roxane felt something prick at the back of her eyelids. 'What was that, Gareth?' she whispered, as hope, wild and unbelievable, stirred somewhere deep inside her.

Gareth reached towards her and put his arm across the sheet where he thought her waist might be. 'It meant I loved you, Roxane. I think I've loved you almost from the beginning—but—I was too arrogant to believe it. Because once I was past childhood everything that happened to me happened because I made it. And I decided years ago that Annette and I should marry. It never occurred to me that I could have made a mistake.' He pushed his hand through his hair, and added with heartfelt conviction, 'God, *what* a mistake.'

'Yes,' agreed Roxane. 'When you do things, you do them on a grand scale, don't you?' She closed her eyes and tried not to believe that she had heard him say he loved her. She mustn't let herself hope. Not yet. Because it would hurt too much if that hope was shattered again. So she stirred uncomfortably under the weight of his arm, wishing he would move it and yet glad that it was there. And quietly, almost as if talking to herself, she fastened on his words which meant the least.

'I never did understand what it was you saw in Annette,' she murmured musingly.

He rolled his head back on the pillow and stared up at the ceiling. 'She was an old and trusted friend. And she had certain other—obvious attractions.'

'I know that, but . . .'

'And she's not really as useless as you think. If you saw her in her own environment, manipulating figures instead of people, you'd see that she has her good points.'

'I suppose so. Maybe I'm just jealous.'

'You needn't be.'

Roxane opened her eyes to gaze down at him. 'Is that true, Gareth? You're really not married to Annette?'

He smiled, a slow, tender, utterly irresistible smile. 'You still don't trust me, do you?' he said softly. 'Yes, it's true. Because when I realised, too late, that if I couldn't have you I must spend the rest of my life alone rather than live a lie with someone else—I cancelled our wedding plans.'

'Why—why did you think you couldn't have me?' Her voice was a whisper, hardly stirring the air.

Something dark and bitter flashed swiftly across his face. 'Because I knew how much you despised deception. Your candour and honesty, your openness, were so much a part of you that I was sure you could never forgive me for not being open with you. For making love to you at the same time I was engaged to someone else. That's why I lost my temper and behaved like such a—what was it you called me?'

'Bastard,' said Roxane succinctly, her amber eyes very bland.

He lifted a finger and ran it along her cheek. 'Yes, that was it. And apart from my own perceptions about you, there was also the little matter of that parting speech of yours.'

'Parting speech?'

'Mm. Don't call, don't write, don't come near me. Ever. You sounded as if you meant it. Remember?'

'Yes, I remember. But Gareth—when I said that—*you* still meant to marry Annette.'

'Did I?' He sat up suddenly, and realised that Roxane was still clutching the sheet about her shoulders. Very gently he pulled it down, leaving her exposed and vulnerable in her thin blue cotton gown. 'I don't know what I meant to do, at that moment, Roxane.' He wrapped a lock of her hair around his knuckles. 'I felt so bloody guilty . . .'

'I know. So you stamped around your apartment like a madman, got me into as bad a mood as yourself—and then told me about your wedding.'

'That's about it. And you called me all sorts of names, didn't believe I was telling you the truth, and generally made me want to hit you. I almost hated you then, because you couldn't see I cared.'

'How could I believe you? You said you loved *me*—but were going to marry Annette.'

Gareth's eyes darkened for a moment and he gazed stonily out of the window. 'I know. I was horribly confused, and the only thing I could hang on to was that I had made a promise, and that promises ought to be kept. I'd seen enough of them broken—by my father. It took me time, and some cool, clear thinking before I realised I was doing no one a favour by embarking on a marriage without love. Buy by then I was sure I'd lost you.'

Roxane didn't answer for a while. When she did speak it was to say slowly, and without apparent connection, 'Poor Annette.'

Gareth shook his head dismissively. 'Oh, it's not as bad as you think. She's not heartbroken. My arrangement with her was not a love-match. We were used to each other, I wanted someone to look after my house and have my children. She wanted comfort and security . . .'

'And now she has neither.'

He smiled ruefully. 'She has, actually. I'm afraid guilt made me recompense her rather handsomely. In fact, she's now the proud owner of my solid pink house.'

'I'm glad.'

'I don't blame you. It's an exceptionally putrid pink.'

'I didn't mean that . . .'

He laughed. 'I know you didn't. You're a generous

woman, Roxane. It's another of the reasons I love you.' He curved his hand deliciously around the back of her neck. 'But right now you look as lovely and unattainable as the moon.'

'Unattainable?'

He stared at her, a long, penetrating stare, almost as if he couldn't quite trust his ears. Then his face lit suddenly with a fierce inner joy as he turned towards her, took both her hands in his and said quietly, 'I love you, Roxane. More than you'll ever know. Will you do me the honour of becoming my wife?'

At these oddly formal words, spoken by this rough, restless and maddeningly informal man—words which she had given up all hope of hearing—Roxane felt a lump stick irritatingly in her throat, and the pricking behind her eyelids erupted unexpectedly into a flood. But she managed to lift her streaming eyes to his.

'Yes, please,' she choked through her tears. 'Yes, darling Gareth. I'd like that very much.'

Gareth's eyes were bewildered as he stroked the soft brown hair cascading over his shoulder, while Roxane sobbed her heart out against his naked chest. He glanced quickly at her back to see if her cut might be hurting her, but the plaster had come off and it really was just a scratch.

'What is it?' he asked, as her sobs became quieter. 'You don't have to cry about it, sweetheart. Being married to me won't be that bad, will it? I know I'm not the easiest man in the world to get along with. But I do love you, Roxane. And I'll do everything I can to make you happy.'

Roxane's hands tightened on his shoulders and she raised her brimming eyes to his face. 'I'm s-sorry,' she whispered. 'I don't know why I'm crying. It's just that I'm so h-happy.'

Gareth patted her awkwardly. 'You cry when you're angry too, don't you? I guess it makes some sort of sense.' He sounded doubtful.

'No, it doesn't.' Roxane's lips parted in a sudden dazzling smile. Her face was still damp, but her eyes were filled with laughter now, instead of tears. 'Nothing makes sense, does it? All my life I've dreamed that when the man I loved asked me to marry him, we'd be somewhere very romantic—like the top of a mountain or by a waterfall, and he'd go down on one knee and look moonstruck and I'd breathe "yes" very soulfully and drift into his arms. Instead of which we're sitting in this rumpled bed, feeling rather the worse for last night—at least I am—in a house with very little furniture—and when you asked me to marry you, instead of looking soulful I burst into tears.'

'Never mind.' He raised her fingers to his lips and kissed them one by one. 'All is not lost. You can still drift into my arms.'

'You're laughing at me,' Roxane accused him. Then she grinned. 'But I guess I can't blame you, can I?'

'No, you can't. Come on, drift.'

Laughing, Roxane put her arms around his neck as he held her tenderly against his chest. Then he kissed her, slowly and very thoroughly.

'Much as I'd prefer to do other things,' he said presently, 'I still think we have to talk. You stay here, my love, and I'll get us a cup of coffee.'

'All right.' She smiled at him. 'And then?'

'And then I'll try to convince you that I'm not the opportunistic villain that you think me.'

'Yes? And then?'

He grinned suggestively. 'And then—I'm open to

indecent suggestions.'

'I never make indecent suggestions,' Roxane called after him as he left.

'You don't? We'll have to see about that.'

Ten minutes later he was back with two steaming cups of coffee which he settled on the table at Roxane's side of the bed. She saw that his chest was enticingly bare, but he was still wearing the jeans he had arrived in last night. From the waist down he was quite respectable. So he really had been the perfect gentleman—for once.

He sat down on the bed beside her, not touching her now but looking into her eyes.

'I owe you an apology—and an explanation,' he said gravely.

She frowned. 'Yes? You mean . . .'

'I mean about why I came back to Vancouver to lay a ghost . . .'

'And ended up finding me instead?'

'Harpy.' He patted her playfully on a bare thigh which was protruding interestingly from under the rumpled sheets. 'As I remember it, it was the other way around.'

'Mm.' Roxane put out her hand and stroked his face. 'I suppose it was in a way. But you see—I thought you were leaving me for ever. I wasn't sure why—but I knew you were going—and I wanted something, even just one night, to remember.'

He heard the slight catch in her voice, and felt something tight and painful tug suddenly at his heart. 'I know,' he murmured huskily, putting a protective arm around her shoulders. 'I know, and I never meant to hurt you, sweetheart. But I wanted something to remember too. That night with Toby, when I knew I loved you—I just couldn't bear to say goodbye. Not again. Not then. I still thought I had to marry Annette, though. You see—I saw my mother suffer from so many broken promises, and it took me a long time before I understood—that Annette could suffer just as much or more if I married her. Not from broken promises, but from lack of love, because one day she might find that comfort and security were not enough.' He swung his legs up beside Roxane's and they sat quietly for a moment before he went on steadily, 'As each day with you passed, and I couldn't bring myself to end it, I found I loved you more and more. And it became harder and harder to speak. I knew I had to tell you. But when I finally did, it came out in the cruellest way possible—cruel to both of us I suppose. We weren't even left with memories of a fond and romantic farewell.'

'No,' agreed Roxane, nestling her head on his shoulder. '*I* was left with memories of you crowing, with a nasty, smug sneer on your face, that you'd come all the way to Vancouver to seduce me.'

'I wasn't crowing.'

'You were. I wanted to hit you.'

'You tried to. And don't ever try it again.'

'I won't,' promised Roxane, smiling.

Gareth ran a finger down her nose. 'I didn't come to seduce you,' he said softly. 'I was angry when I said that. I wanted to, of course, although I didn't intend to. Then you turned up in that glorious black dress . . .' He paused and slid his hand slowly along her thigh as his dark eyes gleamed down into hers. 'Do you realise we're wasting an awful lot of time?'

Roxane sighed happily and rubbed her face against the morning bristle on his chin as Gareth took her by the wrists and slowly moved his big hands up her arms until they reached her shoulders. Then he drew her trembling body very gently into his arms and placed his lips purposefully over hers.

And they never did drink the coffee.

When the landlord knocked on the door that evening—to inspect the damage and to tell Roxane she must leave at the end of the month—he found both of them sitting sedately at the table. They were tucking enthusiastically into bacon and eggs and looking as if there was nothing remotely odd about eating breakfast at eight p.m.

Roxane beamed at him and promised to pay for fresh paint. Gareth gave him a conspiratorial grin and said he needn't worry because he would be removing the problem at the end of the week in any case.

'I'm going to marry her, you see,' he announced complacently.

The landlord wandered off shaking his head and muttering that Gareth must be mad.

'I'm not a problem,' Roxane objected mildly. 'And what do you mean, you're removing me at the end of the week?'

'I have to go back to Toronto. My involvement with you has had a very demoralising effect on my staff. They're under the entirely mistaken impression that I more or less live in Vancouver, and that they can expect to put up with only occasional interference from the boss. I aim to correct that impression.'

'Oh. And where do I fit in?'

'You're coming with me, of course.'

'Well—yes. Eventually.' She sighed. 'Back to snow and cold winters, after all. But Gareth, I do have to settle things here first. I can't just leave Mr Ryerson in the lurch. And there's packing to do, friends to say goodbye to . . .'

He shook his head. 'No need to say goodbye. We'll be back often, especially in the winter for skiing. And you don't have anything to pack.' He waved his hand disparagingly at the still sparsely furnished room.

Roxane sighed again. 'And what about Mr Ryerson? Doesn't he deserve some consideration?'

Gareth grinned. 'No. From now on I hold a monopoly on your consideration.'

'Oh no, you don't.'

It took Roxane fifteen minutes of fast talking, during which her eggs went cold, to convince Gareth he was wrong, and that this time he was not getting his own way. But in the end he was reluctantly forced to agree that perhaps, just perhaps, mind you, she had a point.

'You can come out here at the end of the month,' she informed him practically. 'I'll have everything arranged for our wedding by then, and afterwards we can travel back to Toronto on your beloved train. One of your brothers can be best man, and Nina can be my bridesmaid . . .'

Gareth raised his eyebrows. 'I'm having second thoughts,' he groaned. 'Your impossible friend will probably turn up in scarlet and green polka dots with a pink-striped hat and carrying a bouquet of yellow lupins down the aisle.'

'I like lupins,' laughed Roxane. 'Especially yellow ones. And I thought you and Nina had decided to bury the hatchet.'

'Mm.' Gareth picked up his fork and stabbed it absently at a crumb of bacon. 'You're right, really. If it wasn't for Nina, I wouldn't be here.'

'You wouldn't?'

'No. You know she wrote to me. She told you.'

'Yes—but—what did she say exactly?'

'She said, with her inimitable charm, that although she was allergic to snakes, something you had told her made her think that perhaps I was capable of being human—and that if I cared for you even a little bit, would I please come back and knock some sense into your dizzy head. Because everyone else had tried and failed, and I was her last resort.' He smiled wryly, put down his fork and leaned back in his chair. 'And as I cared for you rather more than a little, I took the next plane out—only to find you cavorting in the arms of your cowboy.'

'I wasn't cavorting. And he was *not* mine.'

'Maybe not. But I could have killed him anyway.'

Roxane had no doubt he could. 'Tell me,' she said slowly, 'if Nina hadn't written, would you ever have come back?'

His eyes darkened. 'On business, yes. To see you, no. You were pretty definite about not wanting me to. And I believed you.'

'That was just because I was hurt and angry.' She hesitated, and brushed a non-existent crumb from her slacks. Then she went on quickly, 'And if you *had* married Annette and then got that letter from Nina—would you still have come?'

Gareth was silent, staring at the rain through the window. Then he shifted his position, crossed one leg over his knee and shook his head. 'No,' he said bleakly. 'No, I wouldn't. I saw what my dad did to my mother, and I vowed a long time ago that if ever I got married, the pattern would not, under any circumstances, be repeated. If I'd married Annette, it would have been for keeps.'

Roxane closed her eyes. 'I'm so glad you didn't,' she whispered.

'So am I.' She felt his fingers touch her cheek and then trail sensuously around her neck. 'Remember I told you once that I would never belong to anyone?'

Roxane nodded dumbly.

'Well, it wasn't true. Because for as long as you want me, Roxane, I'll always belong to you.'

Roxane's sweet face glowed radiantly. 'I love you, Gareth,' she said softly. 'I'll always want you. And I'll always belong to you, too.'

There was no answer when Nina tapped lightly on Roxane's door the following afternoon. She glanced up then and saw that there was a note pinned near the handle. It said simply, 'Thanks, Nina. Wedding at the end of the month. With love and gratitude from The Snake.'

Nina let out a whoop of glee and ran two steps at a time down the stairs to throw her arms ecstatically round the neck of a waiting Jack. It was only with great difficulty that he prevented her from toppling both of them in a tangled heap on the grass.

Miles away up the Squamish Highway, Roxane and Gareth stood beside Shannon Falls.

His arm was around her waist as they stood on a wooden bridge beneath overhanging trees and watched the water stream down over the rocks. The top of the fall was so high up that it was lost among the greenery. A bird was singing somewhere close, but its voice was muted by the roar of water. Dust flaked over them in a golden sunbeam which lit up Roxane's eyes.

Gently Gareth turned her to face him and there was a teasing smile on his lips as he shouted above the roar, 'I couldn't manage a mountain, sweetheart. Will a waterfall do instead?'

Before Roxane realised what he was about, he had taken her fingers in his hand and gone down on one knee. With his mouth quirking suspiciously, he raised his head and said gravely, in a deep, sincere voice from which the laughter was almost, but not quite banished, 'Will you marry me, dearest Roxane?'

Roxane eyed him repressively. 'Don't be an idiot. You know very well I will.' She glanced down the narrow pathway leading to the bridge. 'And there's a party of three teenagers, four kids, a father and two dogs about to invade our privacy. I think you had better get up.'

Gareth rose easily to his feet, and Roxane thought for the hundredth time how beautifully he moved. 'I thought you wanted a romantic proposal,' he grumbled. 'I found you a waterfall, tried to look moonstruck, went down on one knee—and you're not even gazing soulfully into my eyes.'

'No,' replied Roxane drily, 'I'm gazing at that dog on the picnic table. He's about to eat our lunch.'

'To hell with lunch.' Gareth put both hands on her shoulders and drew her purposefully towards him. 'Do I have to do *all* the work?' he wondered. 'You're supposed to be drifting gracefully into my arms.'

With a sigh of happiness Roxane kept her part of the bargain—and as Gareth's lips found hers in a kiss that sealed it for ever, the dog, with a grunt of approval, sat down to gobble up their lunch.

# Harlequin Presents

## Coming Next Month

**1199  THE ALOHA BRIDE  Emma Darcy**
Robyn is at a low point in her life and is determined not to be hurt again. Then she meets Julian Lassiter. Somehow she finds herself wanting to solve Julian's problems in a way that is not only reckless but is positively dangerous!

**1200  FANTASY LOVER  Sally Heywood**
Torrin Anthony's arrival in Merril's life is unwanted and upsetting, for this shallow, artificial actor reminds her of Azur—the heroic rebel sympathizer who'd rescued her from cross fire in the Middle East. Could she possibly be mixing fantasy with reality?

**1201  WITHOUT TRUST  Penny Jordan**
Lark Cummings, on trial for crimes she's innocent of, hasn't a chance when she is faced with James Wolfe's relentless prosecution. Then the case is inexplicably dropped. She wants to hate this formidable man, but finds it impossible when fate brings him back into her life!

**1202  DESPERATION  Charlotte Lamb**
Megan accepts a year apart from her newfound love, Devlin Hurst—she'll wait for him. Yet when her life turns upside down just hours after his departure, she knows she must break their pact. Only she has to lie to do it.

**1203  TAKE AWAY THE PRIDE  Emma Richmond**
Toby lies about her qualifications to become secretary to powerful Marcus du Mann—and is a disaster. But when Marcus gets stuck with his baby nephew, Toby is put in charge. And she's coping well—until Marcus decides to move in and help...

**1204  TOKYO TRYST  Kay Thorpe**
Two years ago, Alex walked out on Greg Wilde when she discovered he was unfaithful. Now they're on the same work assignment in Japan. Despite Greg's obvious interest in the beautiful Yuki, Alex finds herself falling in love with him all over again!

**1205  IMPULSIVE GAMBLE  Lynn Turner**
Free-lance journalist Abbie desperately wants a story on reclusive engineer-inventor Malacchi Garrett. Then she discovers the only way to get close to him is by living a lie. But how can she lie to the man she's falling in love with?

**1206  NO GENTLE LOVING  Sara Wood**
Hostile suspicion from wealthy Dimitri Kastelli meets Helen in Crete, where she's come to find out about the mother she never knew. What grudge could he hold against a long-dead peasant woman? And how would he react if he learned who Helen is?

Available in September wherever paperback books are sold, or through Harlequin Reader Service:

In the U.S.
901 Fuhrmann Blvd.
P.O. Box 1397
Buffalo, N.Y.  14240-1397

In Canada
P.O. Box 603
Fort Erie, Ontario
L2A 5X3

## *Harlequin American Romance*®

*Gull Cottage*

The sun, the surf, the sand...

One relaxing month by the sea was all Zoe, Diana and Gracie ever expected from their four-week stay at Gull Cottage, the luxurious East Hampton mansion. They never thought that what they found at the beach would change their lives forever.

Join Zoe, Diana and Gracie for the summer of their lives. Don't miss the GULL COTTAGE trilogy in Harlequin American Romance: #301 CHARMED CIRCLE by Robin Francis (July 1989); #305 MOTHER KNOWS BEST by Barbara Bretton (August 1989); and #309 SAVING GRACE by Anne McAllister (September 1989).

GULL COTTAGE—because one month can be the start of forever...

GULLG-1

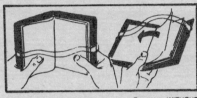

# Harlequin Regency Romance™

## Romance the way it was *always* meant to be!

The time is 1811, when a Regent Prince rules the empire. The place is London, the glittering capital where rakish dukes and dazzling debutantes scheme and flirt in a dangerously exciting game. Where marriage is the passport to wealth and power, yet every girl hopes secretly for love....

Welcome to Harlequin Regency Romance where reading is an adventure and romance is *not* just a thing of the past! Two delightful books a month.

Available wherever Harlequin Books are sold.

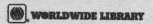

# SWEEPSTAKES RULES & REGULATIONS

## NO PURCHASE NECESSARY TO ENTER OR RECEIVE A PRIZE

1. To enter and join the Reader Service, check off the "YES" box on your Sweepstakes Entry Form and return to Harlequin Reader Service. If you do not wish to join the Reader Service but wish to enter the Sweepstakes only, check off the "NO" box on your Sweepstakes Entry Form. Incomplete and/or inaccurate entries are ineligible for that section or sections(s) of prizes. Not responsible for mutilated or unreadable entries or inadvertent printing errors. Mechanically reproduced entries are null and void. Be sure to also qualify for the Bonus Sweepstakes. See rule #3 on how to enter.

2. Either way, your unique Sweepstakes number will be compared against the list of winning numbers generated at random by the computer. In the event that all prizes are not claimed, random drawings will be held from all entries received from all presentations to award all unclaimed prizes. All cash prizes are payable in U.S. funds. This is in addition to any free, surprise or mystery gifts that might be offered. The following prizes are offered: *Grand Prize (1) $1,000,000 Annuity; First Prize (1) $35,000; Second Prize (1) $10,000; Third Prize (3) $5,000; Fourth Prize (10) $1,000; Fifth Prize (25) $500; Sixth Prize (5,000) $5.

   * This Sweepstakes contains a Grand Prize offering of a $1,000,000 annuity. Winner may elect to receive $25,000 a year for 40 years without interest; totalling $1,000,000 or $350,000 in one cash payment. Entrants may cancel Reader Service at any time without cost or obligation to buy.

3. Extra Bonus Prize: This presentation offers two extra bonus prizes valued at $30,000 each to be awarded in a random drawing from all entries received. To qualify, scratch off the silver on your Lucky Keys. If the registration numbers match, you are eligible for the prize offering.

4. Versions of this Sweepstakes with different graphics will be offered in other mailings or at retail outlets by Torstar Corp. and its affiliates. This promotion is being conducted under the supervision of Marden-Kane, Inc., an independent judging organization. By entering this Sweepstakes, each entrant accepts and agrees to be bound by these rules and the decisions of the judges, which shall be final and binding. Odds of winning in the random drawing are dependent upon the total number of entries received. Taxes, if any, are the sole responsibility of the winners. Prizes are nontransferable. All entries must be received by March 31, 1990. The drawing will take place on or about April 30, 1990 at the offices of Marden-Kane, Inc., Lake Success, N.Y.

5. This offer is open to residents of the U.S., United Kingdom and Canada, 18 years or older, except employees of Torstar Corp., its affiliates, subsidiaries, Marden-Kane and all other agencies and persons connected with conducting this Sweepstakes. All Federal, State and local laws apply. Void wherever prohibited or restricted by law.

6. Winners will be notified by mail and may be required to execute an affidavit of eligibility and release, which must be returned within 14 days after notification. Canadian winners will be required to answer a skill-testing question. Winners consent to the use of their name, photograph and/or likeness for advertising and publicity in conjunction with this or similar promotions, without additional compensation.

7. For a list of our most current major prize winners, send a stamped, self-addressed envelope to: Winners List, c/o Marden-Kane, Inc., P.O. Box 701, Sayreville, N.J. 08871.

---

If Sweepstakes entry form is missing, please print your name and address on a 3″ × 5″ piece of plain paper and send to:

In the U.S.

Sweepstakes Entry
901 Fuhrmann Blvd.
P.O. Box 1867
Buffalo, NY 14269-1867

In Canada

Sweepstakes Entry
P.O. Box 609
Fort Erie, Ontario
L2A 5X3